Sabotage at Willow Woods

Read all the mysteries in the

NANCY DREW DIARIES

#1 Curse of the *Arctic Star*

#2 Strangers on a Train

#3 Mystery of the Midnight Rider

#4 Once Upon a Thriller

#5 Sabotage at Willow Woods

And coming soon

#6 Secret at Mystic Lake

Nancy Drew DIARIES™

Sabotage at Willow Woods

#5

CAROLYN KEENE

Aladdin

NEW YORK   LONDON   TORONTO   SYDNEY   NEW DELHI

This book is a work of fiction. Any references to historical events, real people, or real places are used fictitiously. Other names, characters, places, and events are products of the author's imagination, and any resemblance to actual events or places or persons, living or dead, is entirely coincidental.

ALADDIN

An imprint of Simon & Schuster Children's Publishing Division

1230 Avenue of the Americas, New York, NY 10020

First Aladdin paperback edition January 2014

Text copyright © 2014 by Simon & Schuster, Inc.

Cover illustration copyright © 2014 by Erin McGuire

All rights reserved, including the right of reproduction in whole or in part in any form.

ALADDIN is a trademark of Simon & Schuster, Inc., and related logo is a registered trademark of Simon & Schuster, Inc.

NANCY DREW, NANCY DREW DIARIES, and related logo are trademarks of Simon & Schuster, Inc.

Also available in an Aladdin hardcover edition.

For information about special discounts for bulk purchases, please contact Simon & Schuster Special Sales at 1-866-506-1949 or business@simonandschuster.com.

The Simon & Schuster Speakers Bureau can bring authors to your live event. For more information or to book an event contact the Simon & Schuster Speakers Bureau at 1-866-248-3049 or visit our website at www.simonspeakers.com.

Interior designed by Karina Granda

Cover designed by Karin Paprocki

The text of this book was set in Adobe Caslon Pro.

Manufactured in the United States of America 0318 OFF

8 10 9

Library of Congress Control Number 2013948654

ISBN 978-1-4424-9392-6 (pbk)

ISBN 978-1-4424-9393-3 (hc)

ISBN 978-1-4424-9394-0 (eBook)

Contents

Dear Diary,

I THINK GEORGE'S COUSIN CARRIE KIM has gotten way more than she bargained for with her city council campaign. Bess, George, and I are really worried! She thought her platform of building a new sports field and complex would be a slam-dunk, but it turns out some people are really upset.

Now that someone is threatening her, I know it's up to me to solve this case, even if that means going undercover at a different high school. I should probably go brush up on my environmental knowledge if I'm ever going to be believable as a member of the Green Club. . . .

CHAPTER ONE

The Wrong Message

"OOH, ANOTHER COTTON-CANDY SELLER!" My best friend Bess leaned back and craned her neck, pointing down the sidewalk to a middle-aged man surrounded by wispy puffs of yellow and blue— the Boylestown Raiders colors. We were attending a parade and block party to celebrate Boylestown's football team winning the state championship. Bess, her cousin George, and I all went to a rival school—River Heights High—so why were we celebrating with the competition? Well, George's cousin, Carrie Kim, had decided to run for Boylestown's town council, and she was making her first big speech at the block party. We all wanted to be there to show our support.

"I don't need another cotton candy," George, who was my other best friend, muttered with a frown. "I'll puke."

Bess turned back and shot George an annoyed glance. Bess is as blonde, curvy, and lively as George is dark, petite, and serious. Over the years, I've become very good at refereeing their arguments.

I held up a hand. "Now ladies . . ."

"You don't need to be such a grump." Bess frowned at George and looked down the street to where a parade would be starting any minute.

"I'm *not* being a grump." George sighed, following Bess's gaze to where the Boylestown High School band was getting into formation. "I think it's great that the Boylestown football team won the state championship. And I think it's great that the town is coming together to give them this parade."

I cocked an eyebrow. I knew what was coming next. "But . . ."

George looked flustered. *"But,"* she repeated, shrugging, "I just wish towns like this would pay the same kind of attention to *other* accomplishments."

I smiled sympathetically. I knew that George was speaking from her own experience as a nonathlete.

"Non-sports-related accomplishments," Bess filled in, and then shook her head. I could tell she'd heard this argument before.

One of the drummers in the marching band banged her drum, and we all looked over to see the band members begin marching in place. The parade was starting! The band began playing, and I could feel my heart beating in time with the *thump-thump-thump* of the drum. What is it about fight songs? They were playing Boylestown High's, and even though I never went to school there, it still made me want to jump up and down and cheer.

As the band marched past us, I saw George straighten up and begin cheering. I knew my friend was really excited about the football team's win, deep down. I cheered too, clapping along to the beat of the song. The crowd suddenly erupted in hooting and applause, and I turned to see that the football players themselves were behind the band, each wearing his uniform and carrying his helmet in his hands. Bess stuck her fingers in her mouth and let out her famous Brain-Melting Whistle. George rolled her eyes and rubbed her temples, but notably didn't tell her cousin to stop.

The Boylestown cheerleaders followed the players, but after them, the parade petered out. A few little kids marched by, waving pompoms or flags, but I had a feeling they were an unofficial addition to the parade. This hunch was proven when a few middle-aged parent-looking types scurried by just seconds after, trying to round up the kids.

"That's it?" George asked. "The band and the football team?"

"And the cheerleaders," Bess corrected her, pulling some pink lip gloss out of her pocket and applying a perfectly shiny coat. I couldn't help being impressed—how did she put it on so perfectly without a mirror?

But I knew I shouldn't have been surprised. Bess was an expert on all things clothing-, makeup-, or style-related. She would have been a total girly-girl, if she weren't also an amazing mechanic.

George let out a puff of breath and ran a hand through her short, straight black hair. George's interest in makeup or style ran directly inverse to her cousin's; she couldn't care less. What she did care about was technology. It seemed to me that George could do *anything* with a computer: order up dinner, animate a short film, listen in on a conversation taking place across the world. She was also very concerned with justice and fairness. Which made her incredibly useful to me in following my own passion: catching crooks.

"Come on, guys, let's get moving," Bess said, gesturing to the stream of people flowing into the street to follow the parade down to the school grounds, where a block party would soon take place. We moved into the crowd. All around us, I could hear snippets of conversation. I didn't mean to snoop, exactly—it was just habit.

"—such an *amazing* team—"

"—really incredible, it's been twelve years since BHS even made it to state!"

"—I know—they're *heroes*!"

At those words, I heard George snort. She turned to face me, and I could tell from her expression that she'd definitely heard the same snippets.

"Heroes?" George asked the willowy redhead who'd used the word. "For getting a ball down a field?"

The girl turned to face George. She was a few inches taller, and peered with large green eyes down her narrow nose at this unexpected interrupter. "It's not that easy," the girl retorted with a sniff. "I'd like to see *you* try it."

"Well, I'd like to see *you* write a 3-D animation program in C++!" George cried.

The girl frowned. "I don't know what that even means," she muttered, before walking away and disappearing into the crowd.

George kept staring at the place where the girl had stood. "Exactly my point!" She turned back to me and Bess and, seeing our faces, sighed. "Look, guys, I don't want to ruin a fun day. It's just—it's just—"

"Not everybody plays sports," Bess said in a slightly bored tone. Bess herself was quite the field hockey champ. It hadn't been long since she'd brought home her own state championship trophy.

"That's true," said George, "but almost everybody does something exciting that deserves attention. Did you know the Boylestown chess team is ranked among the top chess teams in the *country*?"

That surprised me. "I didn't know that," I said, feeling a little bad that I hadn't. "That's really cool."

"It *is* cool," George agreed. "And it takes hard work. But nobody's giving those kids a parade."

I bit my lip and glanced over at Bess. I could tell by her expression that she was thinking about what George had said. But before she could speak, her eyes widened and she stood taller and waved through the crowd. "George—it's Carrie! Hey, Carrie!"

I looked over where Bess was waving and saw George's rosy-cheeked, dark-haired cousin moving gracefully through the crowd. She wore a bright-blue suit with a red-striped blouse, and had a silver eagle pin on her lapel.

"Wow," George said, grinning as her cousin approached. "You really look the part!"

Carrie blushed and grinned back, gesturing to her suit. "Do you like it? Julia, my campaign manager, thinks it's important that I look 'like someone who loves American democracy,'" she said, using finger quotes. A few weeks before, Carrie had told George that she was going to run for town council. George had thought it was a great idea—Carrie was one of her favorite cousins, and she was qualified. She had spent the last three years working for a local congresswoman, and George knew she'd be a great voice for the people of Boylestown.

"I always thought I loved American democracy," George said with a sly grin, gesturing down at her jeans and peasant blouse. "But I guess, as usual, I'm not dressing the right way."

Carrie reached out and playfully pushed her cousin. George smiled. "Hey, so are you ready for your big speech?"

George had told us that Carrie—herself a former tennis champion at BHS—was set to introduce the players at the block party. First she would make a brief speech about her own experience as an athlete there, and her plans for the school, should she be elected.

Carrie took a deep breath. "I sure hope so. I have a major announcement to make today—one that just might help me win this election!"

Bess cocked her head with a smile. "Do tell!" Since Carrie was George's cousin on her mother's side of the family, Bess and Carrie weren't related. But I knew that she was just as impressed by Carrie's politics as George was. All of us knew Carrie pretty well, and growing up, we'd all looked up to her.

Carrie shook her head. "No spoilers! You three will have to find out the big news with everyone else."

George sighed. "No fair! Just whisper it to me. Cousin's privilege."

Carrie grinned. "Learn some patience, little cousin." She reached out and ruffled George's hair before disappearing back into the crowd.

"I *hate* it when she does that." George grimaced, trying to smooth her hair back into place.

I patted her shoulder as we moved to get a good position several yards back from the stage. Already the band was filing into temporary bleachers, having moved on from the school fight song to "America the Beautiful." I watched as Carrie moved through the crowd and stepped up onstage.

The three of us waited patiently as the band played three more songs. Then the Boylestown principal got up and made a speech about how proud she was of the football team, and finally Carrie rose to speak.

"Here we go," George whispered. "The reason we came!"

Carrie moved to the mic and introduced herself. "I'm Carrie Kim, I'm running for town council, and I was also a state champion athlete at Boylestown High—in tennis!"

The crowd went wild. "Boylestown! Boylestown! Boylestown!" a few boys to our right began chanting.

Carrie raised her hand to silence them. "Boylestown

has a history of producing exceptional athletes, because the town values the ingredients that make a great athlete: strength, perseverance, and loyalty."

She paused while the audience cheered.

"But in recent years," Carrie added, "I believe that BHS, faced with some tough budgeting decisions, has let its facilities decline. As a town, we need to do more to support our high school athletes. The football field is in poor shape and on a rocky, uneven field. The bleachers are too small and in poor repair. Even the gymnasium at BHS is out of date. The football team has to work out at the Y, because they don't have adequate facilities at the school."

The football players, who were lined up to go onstage, all nodded their heads in recognition. The crowd let out a few stray boos.

"That's why," Carrie went on, "if I'm elected, the main goal of my first term will be to champion the building of an all-new football field and sports complex at BHS!"

If Carrie said anything after that, I couldn't hear

it—her voice was immediately eclipsed by screaming, clapping, and cheering from what seemed like the entire crowd. Bess was hooting as loudly as anyone else, and even I found myself pretty excited by it all. But then I noticed that George herself was only clapping halfheartedly, and her expression was troubled. I nudged her, and George shook her head. "More money for sports," she whispered to me. "Did you know BHS had to lay off three teachers last year? The town didn't budget enough to pay them."

That dampened my enthusiasm a bit. Was George's cousin making a big mistake? But the crowd was still whooping and cheering. One of the football players ran up onstage and grabbed Carrie in a big bear hug. Carrie pulled away, laughing.

"I hope you'll support my campaign for town council," she went on. "Now, to the real reason we're here: to introduce the State Champion Boylestown Raiders!"

The crowd got loud again, and the awkward moment was forgotten in pure celebration. After about an hour, when the speeches and awards were over, the three of us moved off toward the BHS parking lot, where I'd left my car. George spotted Carrie moving through the crowd too. She seemed to be headed for the parking lot but was making slow progress because people kept stopping her to shake her hand or give her a high five. "Hey, cuz!"

Carrie spotted us and gestured for us to wait for her. A few minutes later—after several handshakes, three high fives, and one kissed baby—Carrie emerged, flushed and looking energized. "Hey, guys! I think that went well, huh?"

"Totally," George said.

Carrie looked down at her hand, where she was clutching a folded piece of paper. "Someone handed me this in the crowd," she said. "I hope it's not some guy's phone number!" She opened up the note and looked down at it, and suddenly her face paled. "Uh-oh," she whispered.

"What is it?" Bess asked. When Carrie didn't respond and just kept staring down at the note, George reached over and took the paper from her cousin's

hand. She tilted the note so all three of us could read
it. I leaned in to get a better look, then gasped.

NOT EVERYONE LOVES SPORTS.
STOP YOUR CAMPAIGN—OR YOU'LL
BE SORRY!

CHAPTER TWO

A Surprise Enemy

CARRIE WENT PALE. "WHAT—WHAT IS THIS?" she asked, turning around as though she expected to find the note writer smiling and waving.

"It's a threat," I said, a note of concern slipping into my voice. "An anonymous one. Unfortunately, politicians get them all the time."

Carrie shook her head, looking back at the note. "I just don't understand," she said. "What I said was so basic. How could it make someone this mad at me?"

"I think the *someone* in question isn't a rational person," George replied, frowning. "And we need to figure out who he or she is, before they act on that threat."

Carrie looked up. Her expression was so vulnerable, it made her look like a little kid. "Nancy," she said, turning to me. "George has told me a lot about the mysteries you've solved. I know you're very smart and resourceful. Will you look into this for me?"

I smiled, taking the note from George and carefully placing it into my purse, trying to preserve the evidence. "I would have tried to catch the creep even if you hadn't asked," I said honestly.

"I hope Carrie doesn't have to suspend her campaign," George murmured later that afternoon, picking at my bedspread with jumpy, nervous fingers. We were all settled in my room, and I held the offensive note in my hand. I was using my own personal kit to dust it for fingerprints. Snooping 101.

"She won't have to suspend her campaign," I said comfortingly. "I'll find whoever wrote this, and we'll figure out what's going on. But it's going to be a little harder than I thought." I put down the brush and pulled over my trash can, shaking the bright-blue powder off the paper and into the trash. "I'm not getting a single print off this thing."

"Ah," Bess said with a knowing nod, "a seasoned threatening-note writer."

I pulled my mouth into a tight line. "Right. Must've worn rubber gloves to write it." That made things a little difficult.

Bess leaned over from where she was lying at the foot of my bed and took the note from me. "The handwriting is pretty standard, huh? Block letters, black marker."

"Yup," I agreed. "No distinguishing marks."

Bess looked closer at the note and frowned. She brought the paper close to her face, then moved to get closer to the reading lamp on the bedside table and turned it on.

George perked up from her seat at my desk. "What do you see?"

Bess tapped her lip with a perfectly polished fingernail. "There's a little bit of a logo here—like this was written on some kind of official stationery."

I leaned over to look, and Bess gestured to the top of the note. Sure enough, a tiny bit of embossed blue ink was visible at the very top—like whoever had written the note had cut off the identifying part of their stationery. It wasn't much to go on, though—just a bit of a circle and the very bottom part of what looked like three letters.

"What letters are those?" George asked. She'd jumped up and was now standing over us, peering down at the note.

"I can't tell." I brought the paper closer to my face, then breathed in and coughed. "Ugh! Well, here's another clue—this reeks of smoke."

Bess sniffed the note and nodded. "Written by a smoker, clearly."

I squinted at what remained of the letters. A curve with a flat bottom, a single line, and double equally spaced lines. I'd looked at enough ripped-up clues in my time to know what the letters might be. "The first one has to be a *B*. The second could be an *I* or a *T*. The last one looks like an *A* or an *H*."

George raised her eyebrows. "*B* for Boylestown?" she asked.

"*A* for Association," Bess suggested.

I looked up. "George, where's your tablet?"

George grabbed her purse and pulled out the latest addition to her gadget arsenal: a small tablet that she ran her finger across to wake up; then she pulled up her browser. "Let me do a search. . . . Boylestown Association. Hmmm." She paused while the search engine did its magic, then read the results. "Boylestown Seniors Association."

"No," I said, frowning down at the note. "The middle letter definitely isn't an *S*."

"Boylestown Fire Safety Association. Boylestown Stamp Collectors Association?"

Beth groaned. "No to both of those."

George read the next entry and looked up, crooking an eyebrow. "Boylestown Teachers Association?"

I looked down at the note again. "That's it! George, go to their home page."

George bent over her tablet and obeyed. "Here we go," she said, lifting the tablet to show us the home page of the Boylestown Teachers Association. A round seal dominated—a seal that seemed to match right up with the tiny bit of circle left on the note in my hand.

"So it stands to reason," I began, "that the person who wrote this note is a teacher at one of the Boylestown schools. And since Carrie is proposing a major change at Boylestown High . . ." I trailed off, but the gleam in Bess's eye told me that she knew exactly where I was going.

"It makes sense to start there," she murmured.

Luckily, RHHS had a teachers' conference the next day, which left me free to begin my snooping. I snuck down into the kitchen while Hannah was dusting the living room, not wanting to answer a bunch of questions about why I was shoving a hastily made peanut butter sandwich into my mouth. Then I grabbed my backpack and jumped into my car, checking my reflection in the mirror. A simple skirt and polo shirt Bess had picked out for me, an artfully messy ponytail: I looked cute enough to blend in, but not cool or noticeable enough to stand out.

I drove quickly to Boylestown High School and parked on a nearby side street. The bell was just ringing for their second lunch period—perfect! Soon the campus was crawling with kids carrying brown paper bags or trays laden with franks and beans, all looking for a place to eat. The school was pleasantly chaotic. Nobody would notice a girl who maybe, if you were really thinking about it, didn't belong.

I walked confidently into the main building, smiling at any kids I passed, like I was just one of them. Most kids smiled back. Nobody asked who I was. I was able to make my way easily down to the basement level, past the cafeteria to the room I was seeking—which was exactly where the map I'd found online had said it would be.

A thick metal door, painted green, held a small

window that had been papered over so you couldn't see inside. *Typical,* I thought. I raised my hand and made a few sharp knocks, my knuckles bumping against the *C* in TEACHERS' LOUNGE.

The door finally swung open to reveal a tall man with longish sideburns and a shaggy mustache. He peered down at me through too-thick glasses, looking instantly annoyed. "This is the teachers' lounge. It's private. No students!" he barked, then pulled back his arm to close the door in my face.

"But wait!" I said, holding up my hand in the universal *please stop!* gesture. "I know the teachers' lounge is private. It's just that I found this lighter right outside the door here—I figured it must belong to someone inside?"

I reached into my pocket and pulled out a small butane lighter I'd bought at the drugstore a few hours earlier. I'd been careful to buy a gender-neutral color: green.

The man frowned, peering down at the lighter. "Hold on." He closed the door again, briefly, while I could hear him talking to the other teachers inside. "You sure? Okay." He opened the door and shrugged at me. "I don't know whose that is. It doesn't belong to any of the teachers in here."

I put on my best *oh gosh* face. "Oh, that's too bad. I'd really like to return it. Do you know any teachers here who smoke?"

The man sighed, as if he were getting tired of this distraction from his rare "me" time. "Which teachers here smoke? Well, there aren't many. It's bad for you, you know that, right?"

I nodded solemnly. Oh, I knew. In fact, my dad had found that it was much easier to quit smoking than to put up with my constant nagging. Win for Nancy Drew!

The man shook his head. "There's . . . uh . . . Ms. Kashen, she still smokes. And Ms. Meyerhoff. You could try them."

"Thanks," I said cheerfully, but barely got the *th* sound out before the door was closed in my face again.

I slipped the lighter back into my pocket and

strolled off, up a flight of stairs. *Ms. Kashen and Ms. Meyerhoff.* I'd have to play dumb when the bell rang again, tell some passing students that I was new and needed to find their classrooms. Of course, I could explore a bit now, see if I happened by them. . . .

As I walked down the hall, I wondered what either of these teachers could possibly get from sending a threatening note to Carrie. Maybe they didn't support her ideas to improve the school, but why threaten her? These were adults, not naive kids. Wouldn't it make more sense to simply not vote for her, or better yet, campaign for one of her opponents? Sending a threatening note was personal. It said, *Not only do I not like your politics, but I'm afraid of what will happen should you win.* But what about Carrie was that threatening? Even a new sports arena was just a new sports arena, not something that could really *hurt* anyone. . . .

As I reached the end of the hallway, loud chanting broke through the usual lunchtime din: "NO NEW ARENA! NO NEW ARENA!" It was coming from a hallway off to the right. *Seriously? It's like they knew I was coming!* I scrambled to follow it.

I ended up back in the BHS lobby. Big trophy cases lined the walls, and a mosaic of the BHS Raiders' logo was laid into the floor. In the middle of the lobby, about twenty kids were marching around in a circle, holding signs that said no NEW SPORTS ARENA! and WE WON'T TRADE TREES FOR TROPHIES!

I moved closer. *These kids seem pretty opposed to Carrie's idea. . . . What is this?*

"Hey." A tall, skinny boy with a messy mop of black hair and a nose ring pressed a flyer into my hand. "Take one of these. Read up! The future of your school depends on it."

I scanned the flyer.

> *. . . but when examined more closely, Carrie Kim's proposal has many areas for concern. Willow Woods, which would be reduced by half to accommodate the new football field, has been undisturbed for more than one*

hundred years, and it contains plant and
animal species that can't be found anywhere
else within thirty miles. . . .

Suddenly I became aware of a shadow looking over me. I looked up and saw the same boy watching me with interest. "It's pretty upsetting, right?" he asked in a much gentler voice than he'd used before.

I nodded, looking down at the paper. "I—I guess I didn't realize the forest was going to be cut down to build the new football field and sports complex," I said honestly. The truth was, all the information in the flyer came as a surprise. I knew that not everybody in Boylestown would support having so much money being funneled into athletics when it could go toward other things. But I hadn't realized there would be environmental concerns.

The boy nodded fervently. "Most people don't!" he said. "People worship sports in this town. It's like nothing else matters. But there's no reason we have to destroy the environment to give something *else* to a bunch of already entitled jocks."

Already entitled jocks. Okay, clearly this boy had a few issue with athletes. *Keep that in mind.* I looked up to meet his pale-green eyes. "Do you think Carrie Kim knows all this?" I asked, waving the flyer. "I know she was an athlete in high school, but . . . maybe she'd change her proposal if she knew it would be so damaging to Willow Woods."

The boy snorted, then seemed to take in my surprised reaction and shook his head. "Sorry, I don't mean to be rude. But I can guarantee you: Carrie Kim only cares about getting elected. All politicians do, when it really comes down to it. That's why it's on the people to stand up for issues we really care about."

I glanced down at the flyer again, pretending to read over a section about the history of Willow Woods, but really just buying some time to think this over. Could the mystery note writer be involved with these environmentalist protesters? Was that enough of a reason to threaten someone—worrying that they would do damage to the environment?

I looked up at the boy and gave him a warm smile.

"I'm Katrina, by the way." Years of snooping around to catch crooks had given me a lightning-fast ability to make up fake names.

He nodded, smiling back and holding out his hand. "Barney."

"That's a nice name," I said. Actually it made me think of a big purple dinosaur. But the Barney I'd grown up watching on TV had little in common with this serious, slight, pale-skinned boy.

"Besides"—Barney leaned toward me, lowering his voice like he was about to let me in on a big secret— "she's one of *them*. She was this huge tennis champ in high school, you know? She was all over the papers. One whole shelf of the trophies over there are hers," he said, nodding to the case. He stood up straight. "Carrie Kim thinks athletics are the answer to everything. They made her life awesome, right? But she doesn't realize that sports actually make some people's lives miserable." He looked down at me, his eyes raw with honesty.

I cleared my throat. "Right," I said, riffing off his comments. "I feel like I always have to feel bad about not being good at running, or shooting a ball through a hoop. But do *they* ever feel bad about not being good at painting? Or gardening?"

The boy nodded. "*Exactly.* Athletes already get everything they want! This is just one more thing."

Barney put a hand on his hip. "So—are you interested in getting more involved, Katrina? We're going to need all the help we can get to mount an effective campaign against Carrie Kim and her big, sports-loving, election-winning idea. And I don't want to get too woe-is-me here, but as a fellow student, I'm sure you know that athletes will always have more power at BHS than the little guy. If they want this new sports complex—well, we're going to have to work really hard to defeat it. Think outside the box a little. Maybe get our hands dirty."

Think outside the box. Get our hands dirty. Each of Barney's words got my little justice-loving inner PI thrumming with enthusiasm. Even if Barney wasn't directly connected to the note Carrie had been passed, I had a feeling I could still learn about a lot of shady activities done in the name of green living. "I'm in," I said, taking his hand and giving it a good shake. Barney winced and pulled away, but smiled at me just the same.

"That's great!" he said, looking like he really meant it.

"So what's the next step?" I asked, holding up the flyer. "Who do I talk to? I'm ready to get my hands dirty!"

"Read the flyer. Think about it. If the ideas resonate with you, then you can start by joining the Green Club," Barney said, grabbing my flyer and writing something on the bottom. "Room 238. You'll need to talk to our faculty sponsor."

"And that is?" I asked, taking the flyer back from him and squinting at the room number.

Barney smiled. "Ms. Meyerhoff," he said. "I hope I see you at our next meeting, Katrina."

CHAPTER THREE

~

Caught on Tape

AS I WAS WALKING BACK TO MY CAR, I GOT A series of texts from George explaining that Carrie had invited us to fill three unsold seats at a big fundraising dinner she was throwing that night. The other attendees would be rich potential donors to her campaign, so the event would be very fancy. WE CAN'T SAY NO, George's last text said.

Well. Who was I to argue?

That night I pulled up to the Boylestown Yacht Club at precisely five thirty, as George's e-mail had instructed. Already the parking lot was buzzing with activity, with well-dressed people climbing out of cars and limos and walking a red carpet to get inside. I watched curiously, smoothing my own simple green dress over my knees. I hadn't been to many fancy fund-raising dinners in my short life, and despite Bess's fashion advice, I wasn't totally convinced I'd dressed the part.

I was pulled from my worries by a sharp rap on my passenger window. It was Bess—expertly made up and wearing a fashionable black cocktail dress, of course. I clicked the unlock button on my door and gestured for her to get into the car. George was right behind her, wearing a red skirt and striped shell, and she pulled open the back door and climbed in.

"You look nice," George observed mildly.

"Do I?" I fingered my hair, which I'd halfheartedly styled with a curling iron. "I'm watching all these people go in and feeling only about thirty percent as fancy as I *should* be to attend this party."

"Oh, come on, Nance." Bess reached over and pinched me. "You look great. And hey, your name even *rhymes* with 'fancy.'"

"Fancy Nancy!" George said, delighted. "Like the picture books!"

I groaned. "Never call me that again, please."

"I'm going to call you that *every day*."

"Can we talk about something else?" I reached into the small purse I'd brought and pulled out the flyer Barney had given me, now folded and creased from multiple readings. I handed it to George. "For example: I think I have a lead on the mystery note writer."

"A lead?" George asked, unfolding the flyer and burying her nose in it.

"Did you go to the school today?" Bess asked. Before they'd left the day before, I'd gone over my plan with my friends. "At lunch?"

"I did," I replied as George flipped over the flyer, making murmuring noises of approval. "And I stumbled onto a protest run by this environmental club, the BHS Green Club, which is already *strongly* opposed to Carrie's plans for a new sports complex and football field."

"For good reason, it sounds like," George added,

finishing up the flyer and passing it forward to Bess. "I had no idea Carrie's plan called for those woods to be half destroyed. In addition to prioritizing sports above anything else, it sounds like this new complex is going to wreak all kinds of environmental havoc."

Bess was reading the flyer now, her brow creased. "I'm *sure* Carrie doesn't know how damaging this would be," she said, the corners of her mouth turning down. "She may love athletics, but she'd never want to damage the environment this way. Maybe there's a work-around?"

"Maybe." I shrugged. "But for right now, my main suspect is one Ms. Meyerhoff—faculty sponsor of the Green Club, and one of the two teachers at BHS who smokes."

"You think *Ms. Meyerhoff* wrote the note?" George asked, incredulous. "Marina Meyerhoff? Nance, have you heard of the Boylestown Shakespeare in the Park program?"

"Yeah," I said, catching George's eye in the rearview mirror. Where was she going with this?

"She runs it," George said. "She won, like, state

Teacher of the Year a few years ago. It was all over the local news. She's possibly the most beloved teacher at BHS. Carrie *still* talks about her poetry lectures."

I frowned at George. "Okay. So she's beloved. Does that mean she could never, ever do anything wrong?"

George pursed her lips but remained silent. So did Bess, folding the flyer carefully back up and handing it to me. Our experience catching crooks together over the years had taught us all that criminals rarely look how you expect them to look. All it takes is for a seemingly normal person to make one dumb, rash decision, and *boom*—criminal.

"Anyway, I don't know for sure yet," I went on, slipping the flyer back into my purse. "It's just a lead. I'll keep digging."

"Thanks, Nancy," George said with a sigh. "It sounds like Carrie can use all the help she can get. Now, shall we walk the red carpet?"

"Oh, I *totally* agree," Julia Jacobs, Carrie's old college roommate, and campaign manager, said with an emphatic nod to the seventysomething Southern-twanged gentleman who sat across the table from us. "Driving your car is an unassailable American right!"

The man nodded emphatically. "As a former oil man, it always disturbs me when towns try to cut down on the rights of drivers. I should be able to drive my car downtown and park it with no hassles!"

They were discussing an issue that was fairly controversial in Boylestown: installing parking meters in the downtown area and putting all proceeds toward the struggling schools.

George pushed a long, green-stemmed baby carrot around her plate and nudged my elbow. "Julia doesn't actually know how to drive," she whispered. "She grew up in Brooklyn. She takes the bus everywhere and thinks everyone should do the same."

I watched in amazement as Julia continued her conversation with the old man, still agreeing that yes, parking meters are big-city foolishness, that part of being an American was being a little in love with your car. Julia worked for a big midwestern PR firm. The way George described it, she was pretty hot stuff, and Carrie was lucky her old friend was willing to take a leave of absence from work to run her local campaign. "Carrie's for the parking meters," George whispered. "Like, hugely, one hundred percent for the parking meters."

That's when something amazing happened. Julia tilted her head to the side, as if something had just occurred to her, and said, "Although . . . there is another way to look at it." I glanced at George, and Bess on her other side, and raised my eyebrows. As we listened, Julia seamlessly laid out the ideas behind Carrie's feelings on the importance of education, and how children are the future, and really, would having to pay fifty or seventy-five cents to park really dissuade people from driving? All the while, she studiously avoided contradicting the old man in any way, or implying that he had said anything wrong. By the end of her speech, the man was nodding vigorously, saying "Oh, yes," like the parking meter plan was obviously the right choice.

Bess looked at the two of us with wide eyes.

"Whew, she's good. Why isn't *she* running for office?" she whispered.

George didn't look quite convinced, though. "Because she lies too much?" she whispered back.

"Of course," Julia was saying now, picking up her wineglass and settling back in her chair, as if this were just a casual fireside chat, "I'm sure Carrie would consider giving other incentives to drivers. The idea is to raise as much money for the schools as possible. Perhaps we cut down on bus service so more people will drive?"

George cleared her throat. She looked like she'd heard enough of Julia explaining what Carrie did and didn't believe. "*Actually*," she said, "I'm pretty sure Carrie would be against cutting bus service in this town. A lot of people rely on it. Also, didn't you tell us that you took the bus here tonight?"

Silence fell over the table, so thick and unexpected, it was like we'd all been covered in glue. Julia turned and looked over at the three of us—as if noticing us for the first time—and clearly did not like what she saw. The older man, who hadn't acknowledged the three of us in any way up to that point, gave George a disapproving look.

Julia pasted on a frozen smile and cleared her throat. "I'm sure you misunderstood my story, George," she said, before waving a vague hand in our direction. "I love to drive. Anyway, have you met Carrie's little cousin and her friends, Mr. Driscoll? Sooooo cute, aren't they? Carrie thought it would be fun to let them come to this dinner and get a little firsthand political education. Of course, they're all too young to fully understand the ins and outs. . . ." She glanced up, and her eyes shot daggers at George. "*George*, would you be a dear and go find the waitress? We need a coffee refill."

George glared at her for a second, but then quickly seemed to remember how much her cousin needed Julia and got up from the table. "Sure thing," she murmured, before disappearing into the crowd. I turned around and shot Bess a look: *Poor George.* She nodded as the conversation continued around us, the three of us forgotten.

A few minutes later, while George was still gone, Carrie stepped up to the podium that had been set up on a raised platform along the inner wall of the ballroom. "Good evening, ladies and gentlemen," she said, and the ballroom erupted in applause. "I wanted to tell you a little bit about how much I love Boylestown—and some of my plans for its future, should I be lucky enough to be elected to the town council."

Carrie paused and took a breath, and George slipped back to our table and sat down. She shot an annoyed look at Julia, but the campaign manager was already focused on Carrie's speech, making a video recording with her phone.

"As I was saying," Carrie went on, "I love this town. When I was just a little girl—"

At that moment, a loud noise came over the sound system—like someone breathing deeply into a microphone. It didn't line up with what Carrie was doing, though, and that was confusing. I glanced at Bess and George, wondering what we were hearing, when suddenly Carrie's voice came booming out of the speakers at a much higher volume than her actual speech. "I DON'T CARE WHAT THEY THINK," the voice, clearly Carrie's, boomed through the speakers, "AS LONG AS THEY CAN AFFORD A TICKET. ONCE I'M ELECTED, I CAN DO WHAT I WANT. I DON'T HAVE TO LISTEN TO A BUNCH OF RICH OLD FOGEYS!"

A stunned silence fell over the crowd, followed immediately by a buzz of angry voices. What was going on? Carrie stopped her speech, looking like a deer in the headlights—where was this coming from?

George was frowning, looking at the nearest speaker. "It's a recording," she whispered. "Somebody's playing it over the sound system."

"But why?" Bess hissed.

"And where did they get it?" I added. "It sounded like Carrie was insulting the kind of rich donors to her campaign who are here tonight!"

George shook her head, looking over at Julia. The pretty redhead had stood up and was craning her neck to look into the back room. She glanced back at Carrie onstage and spread her arms wide, as if to say, *I don't know what's going on—I can't help you.*

Carrie cleared her throat. "I—I—" But as soon as she spoke into the microphone, her voice was drowned out by angry shouts.

"When did you say that, Ms. Kim?"

"When was that recording made?"

"If you really feel that way about your supporters, why are we wasting our time here?"

Carrie shook her head, looking miserable. "I didn't—just give me a minute, please—I can't—"

But people were already beginning to push back from their tables and throw their napkins onto their plates. Angry voices joined in frustration, a kind of chorus of disgruntlement.

"—show *her* what I think about her attitude—"

"—entitled and selfish!—"

"—throw my support behind the *other* candidates—"

Carrie was stunned and silent at the podium. She watched with hollow eyes as many of the guests headed for the door. Even the older man at our table, Mr.

Driscoll, who'd been so concerned about the parking meters, shook his head and got up.

"Please, Mr. Driscoll, don't go," Julia begged, her smile wide but desperate. "Obviously we're having some sort of technical difficulty, but I know Carrie's heart—"

But Mr. Driscoll gave Julia a look of pure contempt. "I'm leaving. At the very least, Ms. Kim has some explaining to do," he said crisply. "I am withdrawing my support until she can explain her statements."

Julia's face fell like an undercooked soufflé. Mr. Driscoll nodded at the carefully styled older woman next to him, and they rose to leave together. Slowly the rest of our table began moving on too. I looked helplessly at Bess and George. It seemed safe to say that the dinner was breaking up.

George squeezed my arm. "Let's go find Carrie," she said.

I didn't argue. I could imagine that whatever had happened tonight, George's cousin could use a sympathetic ear right about now.

Bess, George, and I all made our way to the corner of the platform where Carrie stood, bent over and looking stricken.

"Are you okay?" George asked softly, touching her cousin's shoulder.

Carrie let out a sharp laugh and turned. Her eyes were red with tears.

"I'm very much *not* okay," she whispered, dissolving into a sob. "I don't even know what happened!"

"Someone must have hacked into the sound system to play a recording," George explained.

"Was that recording really you?" Bess asked softly.

Carrie nodded. "That was really my voice," she said. "But those words were taken totally out of context! This was a conversation I had with a few local reporters. The piece you heard was part of a much longer answer about how I'm not going to be swayed by special interests—I want to govern in the best interest of my constituents." She sniffled. "I think it's important for politicians to represent their town fairly—not just the people with money."

"Well, someone got access to that recording and created a totally different message," George said grimly. "Someone with pretty good editing software, because it sounded natural. Usually if you cut and patch dialogue together like that, it sounds choppy."

Carrie shook her head and swiped at her eyes. I followed her gaze across the room, where Julia was chasing down a group of four little old ladies. "—all a *big* misunderstanding!" she was saying. "If you knew the Carrie *I* know—like *I* know her . . ."

Hmmmmmm.

My mind was spinning a mile a minute. So many questions were swirling around in my brain. If Carrie was telling the truth and the recording was taken out of context, who would want to sabotage her campaign like this? Was it the same person who'd written the mystery note? Could this be step one of what the note had promised: YOU'LL BE SORRY? And did it all trace back to worries about the environmental effects of building a new sports complex?

Carrie accepted a tissue Bess offered from her purse

and wiped her face, then noisily blew her nose. She seemed to be trying to pull herself together. "Come on, girls," she said, looking from George to Bess to me. "I want to see something."

Carrie led us through a closed doorway that led to a noisy, hot space. The kitchen lay down a narrow hallway. Just off the hallway was the control room.

Carrie walked over to a large sound system. She reached out, and before I could yell, *Don't touch it—you'll mess up the fingerprints!*, she pulled a tiny flash drive from a USB port.

George held up her hand. "Give it to me," she said. She dug into the black leather tote she'd brought and pulled out her shiny tablet. As soon as Carrie handed her the drive, George had it plugged in and was touching the screen to play the audio file that lay within.

"I DON'T CARE WHAT THEY THINK . . ." Carrie's voice rang out, small and tinny, from the tablet's speakers.

George stopped the recording and looked at me. "Ladies," she said, "I think we've found some evidence."

CHAPTER FOUR

✑

Fishing for a Culprit

WHEN I GOT HOME AFTER THE FAILED fund-raiser, I felt so exhausted that I got into bed right away. I figured I'd be out like a light as soon as my eyes closed. But instead I tossed and turned for an hour, mulling the whole case over in my head: Carrie's sports complex plan. What it would do to Willow Woods. Barney and the mysterious Ms. Meyerhoff, beloved teacher and Green Club sponsor. How effortlessly Julia had bent the truth to win over Mr. Driscoll. And the recording—which Carrie claimed was manipulated—and her face when we'd gone to comfort her after her speech was disrupted.

What was really going on here?

I stared out the window at the willow tree outside my bedroom, the long fronds undulating softly in the night breeze. I wasn't aware of falling asleep, but I must have, because suddenly . . .

I stood in a small clearing surrounded by dense forest. It was pitch dark there—I had a tiny flashlight to light my path—and even though I knew we weren't far from the high school or the road it sat on, it was dead silent.

How had I gotten there? Where was everybody?

"Bess? George?" I called urgently, shining my flashlight in a slow circle around me. "Dad?"

An owl hooted, and when I turned around, Barney was standing right in front of me, his pale skin almost blue in the dull light.

"How did you get here so quickly?" I demanded. I hadn't heard any movement behind me.

Barney just smiled. "I think a better question is, what took you so long? Come on."

He grabbed my hand and pulled me into the trees so roughly I dropped my flashlight. "Wait . . . wait!" I cried. "I lost my—"

Barney turned around, his lip pulled back in a sneer. "You don't need it," he hissed, dragging me farther. "This is important, Nancy. I want you to stand right here."

He knows my real name? *The thought occurred to me after Barney pushed me roughly up onto a tree stump, then disappeared into the darkness.*

"Barney?" I called. "Barney? Where are you?"

"Don't move!" his voice yelled from the darkness, but I still couldn't make him out or tell where the voice was coming from. He sounded angry now. "Really, Nancy, it's the least you can do."

I stood uncertainly on the stump, staring into the darkness. What's the least I can do?

Then I was blinded by an overpoweringly bright light. I let out a cry, but it was lost in the ear-melting roar that suddenly came from behind the light, the sound of a hundred truck engines starting up at once. The light started moving toward me, and I realized what it was: a steamroller! And it was headed right at me!

I screamed again. "Barney!" I tried to scramble off the stump, but it felt like

*my feet were held by heavy concrete. "I'm
stuck here! What do I do? What do I do?"*

*He slipped up next to me then, as
silently and surprisingly as he'd first
appeared. His expression held a terrible
disappointment.*

*"Duh, Nancy," he said, turning to the
oncoming steamroller with a shrug. "Just
tell them to stop."*

I woke up panting, soaked with sweat. The tree
outside my window shifted in the breeze, the leaves
making a soft *shhhh* sound, and it only made me tremble
harder. I glanced at the clock by my bed: 3:24 a.m.

It was just a dream. I settled back against my pil-
lows, trying to calm my jangled nerves. *It can't hurt you.
It was just a dream.*

I tried counting to one hundred, slowing my breathing, imagining myself at the beach—all the things that
usually calmed me down. But nothing seemed to work.

It was just a dream, I told myself again.

But why did it feel so real?

The next day I stumbled through school, tired and irritable, until my last, free period, when I changed my clothes and jumped into my car. I was back at Boylestown High, filled with a new sense of purpose, just as the bell signaling the end of the school day rang. Sure, in real life, Barney had seemed nice enough, and the goals of the Green Club seemed noble and sensible. If Carrie's sports complex really was going to cause irreparable damage, then yes, it made sense to let people know. But the events at last night's fund-raising dinner still turned my stomach. It seemed awfully below the belt to frame Carrie for saying something she'd never really said, robbing of her the chance to explain her views.

As the hallways cleared, I stepped cautiously through the doorway of room 238—sophomore English. "Ms. Meyerhoff?" I asked.

The woman I saw at the desk was not at all what I was expecting for the Green Club advisor and possible note writer. She was soft and round, with slightly frizzy, long brown hair and warm, gentle brown eyes. I realized that in the back of my mind, I'd been imagining some hip, edgy woman with piercings, organic designer clothes, and a punkish haircut. "Can I help you?" she asked, looking up curiously.

I cleared my throat. "Um . . . I hope so."

She smiled encouragingly. "Need some help with Shakespeare?" she asked, organizing some books on her desk. "All the English teachers send confused students my way. Just read it out loud. It always helps. It's amazing how universal the problems seem when you speak the words out loud."

I pulled my laptop out of my backpack. "Actually . . . I'm an intern for the *Boylestown Bugle*. I'm doing an article on the new football field and sports complex that Carrie Kim is proposing. I'm collecting quotes from a sample of teachers. Would you mind chatting for just a moment?"

Ms. Meyerhoff's open expression suddenly closed off, and she sighed and shuffled her books into a messenger bag. "I'm sure you could find more interesting people to talk to, Ms. . . . What was your name?"

"I'm sorry." I put my laptop down on a desk and held out my hand. "Katrina Vicks. And I'm interested in whatever you have to say, really."

Ms. Meyerhoff gave me an appraising look, then shrugged and sat back down behind her desk. "Very well. Can we make it quick, though? I have a dentist appointment in half an hour."

I smiled and sat down at one of the student desks, opening up my laptop. "Great. No problem. Can I ask your name and what subjects you teach?"

She nodded. "Ms. Meyerhoff—Marina—and I teach English and music."

I nodded too and tapped out some notes on the laptop. "And how long have you been at BHS, Ms. Meyerhoff?"

"Twelve years."

A long time. I typed that down as well, thinking that Ms. Meyerhoff had been at BHS long enough to develop some strong opinions.

I looked up. "And—Ms. Meyerhoff—can you tell me honestly, how do you feel about the proposed sports complex?"

Ms. Meyerhoff shook her head and looked down at her sweater, where she pulled at a pilling bit. "Well, honestly? I'm sure it will be nice for the athletes, but I wish that money could be spent on arts education instead. Did you know we had to let two art teachers go last year, because there wasn't enough money? But we have money for a new state-of-the-art sports complex. I know the woman proposing the complex was some kind of sports prodigy when she was a student here. I just wonder about this town's priorities sometimes."

I nodded dutifully and wrote all that down. Then I paused and looked Ms. Meyerhoff in the eye. "So the environment doesn't feature at all in your concerns?"

Ms. Meyerhoff didn't blink. "The environment? What about it?"

I pulled the flyer Barney had given me from my backpack, unfolded it, and handed it to her. "Are you familiar with these conflicts? This flyer was handed out by the Green Club."

Ms. Meyerhoff took the paper from me, glanced down at it, then up at me. "Yes, I am familiar with these. And?"

I cleared my throat. "Are you opposed to the sports complex for the reasons detailed in the flyer?"

She shook her head. "I'm more concerned about what it says about how much this town values sports versus art education." She glanced at her watch. "Is that all? I'm running short on time."

I kept pressing. "But aren't you the faculty sponsor of the Green Club?"

Ms. Meyerhoff stopped short and gave me a curious look. "I'm sorry. What kind of an interview is this?"

I tried to smile. "A thorough one?" I glanced down at my laptop, pretended to type something, and added, "I'm really just hoping to get a wide range of opinions on the proposal, Ms. Meyerhoff."

She stared at me for a moment, bemused. "Yes, I *am* the faculty sponsor for the Green Club, but I have little input—the kids run the club themselves. I'm sure they put a lot of research into this flyer, and it was written by one of my best students. Would you like to talk to her?"

I nodded vigorously, then tried to slow myself down, lest I look insane. "That would be very helpful, yes."

"It's Eloise Stromberg," Ms. Meyerhoff said, then spelled it. "Did you get that?"

"Yes." I typed the name into my notes, then looked up at Ms. Meyerhoff. *She really doesn't seem like an angry note writer,* I reflected. *She seems like someone's kindly, artsy aunt.* "Thank you very much. I hope I didn't make you late to your appointment."

With those words I closed my hand around the flash drive we'd pulled from Carrie's sound system the night before and then dropped it onto the classroom floor with a loud clatter. "Oh no! I'm sorry—could you get that for me, Ms. Meyerhoff?"

I really just wanted to see if the teacher had any reaction to the flash drive—a momentary panic, a quick paling of the skin. But Ms. Meyerhoff just knelt down and grabbed it, then handed it to me. "Okay?"

I nodded sheepishly. "Okay." I was getting the sense this whole visit had been a dead end. I had wasted a perfectly nice teacher's time. And worse, I was no closer to finding out who was sabotaging Carrie's campaign.

"Thank you for taking the time to speak to me, Ms. Meyerhoff," I said, shoving the drive in my pocket and heading for the door. I was in such a hurry to get out of there that I nearly collided with a tall, skinny boy walking in. *Barney!*

"Hey there!" he said, his face lighting up when he looked down and recognized me. "Katrina, right? Hold on, I just need to stick our club dues in Ms. Meyerhoff's desk, and then we can talk."

I turned around and waited while Barney greeted the teacher—he seemed surprised to find her still there—and handed over an envelope filled with bills. Ms. Meyerhoff shot me another curious glance, one eyebrow raised. No doubt she was confused about how I knew Barney. Barney turned to me, his face wide open and smiling. "Anyway, let's get down to business," he said jokingly. "Like, are you going to join the Green Club or what? We could really use you."

I hesitated. "I—well, I've definitely been thinking about it!"

Barney nodded. "Good to hear! Come with me; we can chat about it some more."

I glanced back at Ms. Meyerhoff briefly and nodded my good-bye; she was still regarding me with some suspicion, and I figured it was just as well to have an excuse to get out of there quickly. Barney touched my shoulder and led me out of the classroom into the empty hallway, lined with lockers. There was an echo in the hallway, which made it seem even more deserted.

"What's holding you back?" he asked. "Are there any questions I can answer? Because I really can't see any downside to your joining the Green Club."

I couldn't help smiling. Whatever the Green Club was up to, there was no denying that Barney was sort of charming—in an unguarded, eager-to-please way. "You know what?" I said when I felt we were too far from Ms. Meyerhoff's door to overhear. "You've convinced me. I'm in. Do you know where I could find Eloise Stromberg? Ms. Meyerhoff said I should talk to her about getting involved."

Barney's eyes widened in pleasure and surprise—like even though this was exactly what he wanted, he couldn't believe it was really happening. "Do I?! Katrina, I can take you to her right now. Let's get this party started!"

I blushed for him a little then. So Barney was also a little too enthusiastic. But I still couldn't help liking him. Not in a romantic way—I already had a boyfriend, of course—but like a sweet little brother. I wanted to buy Barney a puppy and let him show me all his favorite eco-friendly toys. I followed cheerfully as Barney thundered down the hall, leading the way toward the BHS gymnasium.

Right before we got to the gym, Barney took a sharp left and led me up a set of stairs. At the top of the stairs was a heavy metal doorway that he pulled open, revealing a big, dark room. He stepped inside, and I followed. There was just enough light for me to make out Barney holding his finger to his lips in the universal sign for *Shhh!*

I looked around and realized we were standing at the back of the audience for a small black-box theater. Most of the lights were off, save a bright spotlight that shone on the girl who stood center stage. She had long, curly dark hair and huge brown eyes, and she was wearing long, feathery earrings and a twisted-folded kind of top that I knew Bess would know the proper name for. She looked exotic and cool. Even though I didn't go to this high school, I felt a little intimidated at the sight of her.

It took me a minute to realize she was in the middle of reciting a poem.

"And then there was only empty earth!"

Her voice thundered through the small space, fueled by anger. It burned from her big, dark eyes, and suddenly she seemed a little scary—like a mother bear whose cub is being threatened.

"Because we has torn all the trees away!

And the earth bled, and the birds all fell

from the sky

For we had taken all their safe places

to perch."

Her voice softened then—sadness crept in.

"And the people realized what a grave mistake they'd made. Thank you."

Scattered applause came from the audience. I looked down and realized that about ten or fifteen kids were seated there, spread among the hundred or so seats. They were a varied assortment of high school types: a couple of goth kids; one short boy with dreadlocks and a vintage Tribe Called Quest T-shirt; a girl with huge, dark-framed glasses and a cute skirt printed with baby deer—definitely a cheerleader. That final one made me do a double take: a cheerleader at a poetry slam?

Barney cleared his throat as the applause died down, and I felt a little trepidation as he waved to get Eloise's attention. "What's up, Barney?" she demanded, in a not entirely friendly tone. We stepped closer, and she looked me over as I came into the light. She pushed her mouth to the side, thoughtful, as Barney led me up onstage.

"I think I have a new recruit!" If Barney noticed Eloise's lack of enthusiasm, he showed no evidence of it. His face was pink and happy, and he gestured to me with the excitement of a spokesmodel on a game show as the host announces, "A BRAND-NEW CAR!!"

Eloise's eyes flipped from Barney's face to mine, her unimpressed expression unchanged. "Yeah?" she asked.

I nodded then; I was feeling the need to pull myself together and stand up to this girl. "That's right," I said. "I wondered if I could talk to you about the Green Club? Ms. Meyerhoff said you're in charge."

Eloise's lip curled. "Talk about what?" she asked. "Either you're green or you're not. If you're not, you have no business being in our club." She paused, giving me a challenging look. "So *are* you?"

I stared at her. "I—what?"

"Are you *green*?" she asked, her eyes bugging in

annoyance. I had the sense that I was only going to get one chance to answer this question correctly. *Why am I so intimidated?*

"Y-yes," I said. "I am. I'm green."

Eloise still looked dubious. I was still dressed in my preppy garb, and she took in my braided headband, my stripy boatneck shirt, my ancient khaki skirt, and my loafers. "Prove it," she said simply, a sardonic grin forming on her face. Then she turned back to the microphone. "Hey, everyone," she said, "we have a new presenter here at our weekly Green Poetry Slam. Her name is—"

She paused and looked at me expectantly. "N— Katrina," I blurted. Man, this girl had rattled me!

"Katrina," Eloise said with a smile, as though the name itself proved something she'd suspected about me. "She really, really cares about the environment, and she wants to share her feelings with us today. Take it away, *Katrina.*"

And with that, she handed me the microphone and pushed me into the spotlight.

CHAPTER FIVE

~

On the Spot

NIGHTMARE. NIGHTMARE. THAT WORD ECHOED in my head on a loop as I squinted into the spotlight, unable to even make out how many people were watching me. Had there been ten people in the audience? Or twenty?

I have a confession to make. I'm a very literal person. I appreciate poetry, but I don't "get" it. I'm really good at dusting for fingerprints, pretending to be someone else, asking pointed questions, and escaping various dangerous situations using unexpected household items.

I am *awful* at public speaking.

Now I took a deep breath. *Just fake your way through it, Nance,* George's voice suddenly sounded inside my brain. It was advice she'd given me anytime I'd had to make a speech in school, or do a presentation, or defend my paper in history class. *You're so good at pretending to be other people when you snoop. So just pretend to be a person who'd be really good at this. It's simple.*

"NIGHTMARE!!" I suddenly shouted into the mic, using a deep, guttural voice I never would have recognized as my own.

"Oil spilling!
Wildlife dying!
Chemicals in our water!
Global warming!
Football players trampling over a
    murdered land!
When will it end, when will it end?!"

Figuring that was enough, and that I'd proven myself, I held the microphone out and then dropped it to the stage with a huge *thump*. A few claps slowly emerged from the audience, as if they weren't totally sure how to respond. After a moment, I heard someone chuckling.

Eloise.

She stepped back up onstage and held out her hand. "Wow," she said, shaking her head. "Okay, to be honest, Katrina, I was just messing with you. You didn't really have to do that." She grinned. "But you sure are committed! Come with, me, kid, we can go to my locker to get some more information."

I nodded and picked up the microphone, setting it back on its stand. "Um, thanks."

I was getting a weird vibe from Eloise. In general, I hate it when people claim to "just be messing" with someone they just met. If you're trying to test or throw off a total stranger, maybe you have something to hide. But at least she was cooperating now. Barney gave me a big high five as we left the theater and followed Eloise down a maze of hallways to her locker. "That was awesome, Katrina!"

I could feel myself blushing. "Thanks."

"How come I've never seen you before?" Eloise asked me as we walked down the hall.

"Oh, I just transferred here," I said as casually as I could. "My dad works for a big bank. We move around a lot," I added.

Eloise stopped and looked at me. "Really? Where did you transfer from?"

"Cleveland," I replied easily. Every made-up character I play in the course of my detective work hails from Cleveland. It makes things easier.

Eloise nodded, seeming satisfied. She finally paused in front of a top locker, long ago painted blue but now showing patches of red and pink, too— previous paint jobs—and spun the dials. Two bumper stickers were stuck to the locker: RESPECT THE EARTH and GO VEGAN!

"Are you vegan?" I asked, more to keep the conversation going than anything else.

Eloise nodded, pulling open her locker and revealing an unholy mess of crumpled papers, textbooks, notebooks, and folders. I couldn't judge, because I wasn't particularly organized either. But it was clear that Eloise wasn't going to find what she was looking for anytime soon.

"Lifelong," she said, shoving a couple of books aside and frowning. "It just doesn't feel natural to me to eat animal products. I mean, what other animal drinks another animal's milk past the age of weaning? It's kind of gross when you think about it, right?"

It did seem kind of weird, when she put it that way. "Yeah, kind of."

Eloise refocused her attention on her locker, and I watched carefully, looking at each paper and book, everything she had posted on the inside locker door. A photo of her with a smiling blond girl, a picture of Ryan Gosling with a lipstick kiss—nothing unusual there.

"I've been thinking of going vegan, but it's hard when my parents aren't," I said, hoping to keep her talking. "Maybe you could give me some pointers?"

"Ooh, that's great," Barney said from behind me.

I turned and saw his now-familiar enthusiastic smile. "Going vegan is a major commitment to the environmental cause!"

Eloise nodded, still fishing in her locker. "The important thing is making sure you still get all the nutrients you need, like protein and iron. You end up eating a lot of beans and nuts. You might need to figure out how to cook, a little. But it's totally doable."

Suddenly her digging shifted a few books back, and a sheaf of papers toppled down from the top and onto the floor. Eloise shoved the books back in and scrambled to grab the papers, but I got to them first.

I turned them over and had to work hard to suppress my gasp. *Boylestown Teachers Association*! Eloise had at least twenty pieces of stationery in her locker! Had she stolen them? And more importantly, did that mean she could have written the note to Carrie?

Eloise grabbed the papers back. "I've got so much stuff in here, honestly, I don't know where half of it came from. But I found the literature I wanted to give you."

She shoved a stapled packet of photocopied sheets into my hands. *So you want to go green!* read the top sheet. *Here's what you should know.*

"Thanks," I said, scanning the first few paragraphs. "This looks really helpful."

Suddenly a sharp, tinny beep sounded from inside my backpack. My phone! Eloise looked at me appraisingly as I dropped my backpack onto the floor and dug it out.

"You know, we're not supposed to have our phones on inside the school," she said, pointing to a poster across the hallway: TURN IT OFF! it insisted, with a photo of a huge cell phone that had to be about twenty years old. "But clearly you're a rebel, Katrina." She smiled. "I like that."

I didn't have much time to process Eloise's words, though, because as soon as I pulled out my phone, I saw a text from George: CRISIS!!! COME TO CARRIE'S HQ PRONTO.

My heart started pounding. *What now?*

"Ah, gotta go," I said, hastily shoving the phone

back into my backpack and hoisting the whole thing over my shoulder. "That's my dad. He's waiting in the car outside."

Barney nodded happily, but Eloise looked down her nose at me and said, "You should really take the bus, you know. Environmentalism 101."

"I know," I said, pasting on an apologetic smile. "Still training the parents, you know how it is. See you guys at the next meeting?"

Eloise started to speak, but Barney cut her off. "Yeah! Give me your number and I'll text you the day and time."

Eloise raised her eyebrows, but I didn't have time to wonder about her reaction. I quickly gave my digits as Barney typed them into his phone. Then I apologized again and said a quick good-bye. "I'll text you!" Barney called after me, but I was already halfway to the door.

It took a while to get to Carrie's campaign head-quarters in downtown Boylestown. I'd gotten completely turned around in the school and forgotten where I'd parked, then had to struggle to find parking in the busy downtown district. It was at least half an hour between the time I got George's text and the time I ran, panting furiously, through the front door of Carrie's headquarters.

When I walked in, Carrie was sobbing hysterically, sitting at a long table along the side of the room and surrounded by George, Bess, and Julia, all of whom seemed to be trying to calm her down.

"What happened?" I asked, leaning against a folding chair as I tried to catch my breath.

Julia glanced up at me coolly and then reached for a box I hadn't noticed on the other side of the table. "Well, we received a disturbing package," she said.

The box was about a foot square, covered in stamps and labels, totally unassuming. Carefully angling it away from Carrie, Julia cracked the top of the box open. When I saw what was inside, my stomach roiled and I had to look away. A cold vise of disgust clutched at my heart. Who would send something so upsetting?

The box contained a dead squirrel. Its eyes were already clouded over, and it had dark, nearly black blood still congealed around its mouth, which was open to reveal jutting, sharp, yellowed teeth.

"There was a note, too," Julia said softly, opening up a folded piece of paper she'd placed on the table. The note was still stained with blood. I peered closer to read it.

This is just the beginning if you don't end your campaign and stop the sports center!

~

CHAPTER SIX

Evil Is Winning

AFTER THE REVULSION PASSED, THE FIRST thought I had was *Maybe I should do some forensic testing on the squirrel.* I had a crude forensic testing kit at home. Maybe if I could figure out a cause of death, I could . . .

My second thought was, *But: gross.* I didn't need to be messing with mysteriously deceased wildlife. The squirrel could have rabies, or worse. Besides . . .

"Have you guys called anybody about this?" I asked, gesturing to the now-closed box.

Julia nodded. "The police are on their way."

"Oh, great." If the Boylestown PD was anything like the River Heights PD, that didn't necessarily mean they'd solve the case. But at least some more official channels could deal with the squirrel.

Carrie sat up then and let out another wail. "It's too much." She sobbed. "This is not what I signed on for by running for office! I just wanted to make a positive change in our town."

"You will, Carrie," George said, rubbing her cousin's shoulder encouragingly. "If you can just stay strong and make it through this rough patch, you know the voters will see who you really are. And once they see that, there's no way they could not elect you!"

Julia moved closer, patting Carrie's arm. "She's right, Carrie. Come on—you're the best man, or woman, for the job. You know that. Block all this out—that's the only thing that matters."

Carrie took a deep, shuddering breath and shook her head. "It's not the only thing that matters. Keeping my sanity matters too! I just wasn't prepared for any of this."

Bess cleared her throat. "Carrie," she said softly,

"if you suspend your campaign, the bad guy wins, and your sports complex will never happen. Is that what you want?"

Carrie looked away. She didn't say anything, but she let out a little whimper.

I took a seat in the folding chair I'd been leaning on. "Carrie, have you heard of any environmental concerns about building the sports complex?"

Carrie turned to me, opening her eyes wide. "Do I know it's not a perfect plan? Sure. There are pros and cons. But I really want to do something to help the athletics program at BHS. I mean, I got *so* much from my time there."

I opened my backpack and fished out the old, creased flyer Barney had given me, then passed it across the table to Carrie, Bess, and George. "I know sports are important to you. But some people are saying that a bunch of old forest will need to be cut down to build the field."

Carrie let out a deep sigh and wiped her eyes. "Oh, I've heard a little about that."

"Could the center be relocated?" asked George hopefully. "Maybe there's a way for everyone to win here. Does the forest *have* to be half-flattened to build the football field?"

Carrie shook her head, pulling her mouth into a tight line. "No," she said, her voice becoming stronger. "For a lot of complicated reasons, having to do with topography, irrigation, and a lot of environmental engineering reasons, the football field would only work in this one particular place—where the forest is now. That's the only affordable solution. It's unfortunate, but I've tried to address it in our plans. We're going to plant a hundred new trees on the existing football field to make up for the trees lost. Isn't that enough?"

Bess and George made encouraging noises, but I stayed quiet. I knew that Barney and Eloise would emphatically say that no, that was not enough. And I could see their point. There's a difference between a hundred-year-old tree growing in a unique forest environment, and a newly planted tree. I could respect that Carrie was trying to address the concerns, but I could also see why the Green Club was still opposing her plans.

George stood and gestured to me and Bess. "Guys—can we talk for a sec?" she asked, gesturing outside. I nodded and stood, telling Carrie and Julia that we'd be right back. George, Bess, and I walked out the door, and George pointed to a bench sitting in a small garden just across the street.

"So," I said, settling down with my backpack at my feet.

"So," George said with a sigh, settling heavily down next to me. Bess sat down next to her and crossed her ankles. "It just gets worse and worse, Nance. I used to be opposed to the sports complex, but the more that happens, the more I feel like I want to support Carrie's plan just to show these yo-yos that they can't bully her!"

I nodded, and Bess frowned sympathetically. "I know Carrie wants the best for the town," I said. "I just hate that whoever's behind this, he or she isn't letting their ideas speak for themselves."

George nodded too, grimly. "They sure aren't.

Listen, I've been using some special software to analyze the voice recording from last night." Before George had given me the flash drive to dangle in front of Ms. Meyerhoff, she'd copied the recording onto her tablet. "Carrie is right—it's definitely been tampered with. There are all these cuts, meaning that whoever made this took out huge pieces of what Carrie was saying to manipulate the message."

"That's terrible," I said, though a little part of me was happy to learn that Carrie had been telling the truth.

"It is terrible," Bess said, shaking her head. "And the worst part is that it worked. About half the donors who attended the dinner last night have cut off their support for Carrie's campaign. She's worried she won't be able to pay her employees this week! Even if we can convince her to keep fighting, I'm not sure the money will hold out much longer."

I sighed deeply. "I hate it when evil is winning," I murmured.

"Me too," said George, picking at a peeling bit of

paint on the bench. "Did you learn anything at the school that might help?"

"Maybe." I pulled the packet of papers Eloise had given me from my backpack and explained what had happened, from the apparent dead end with Ms. Meyerhoff to my off-the-cuff poetry slam—

"Are you kidding?" Bess said, looking at me with apparent delight. "You seriously dropped the mic, Nance?"

I shrugged. "I think so. I'm not sure. Honestly, the whole thing is a blur. But what's important is it seemed to convince Eloise to talk to me. . . ."

I went on, explaining how Eloise had brought me back to her locker—and how a sheaf of BTA stationery had fallen out of it.

"Whoa!" George cried. "Seriously? So the Green Club *is* behind this!"

I sighed. "I'm not so sure," I said. "I haven't had time to think it through. Eloise does seem really passionate, but I still can't really imagine her doing *that*," I said, gesturing back to Carrie's headquarters.

"That's also a pretty mixed message," Bess added, twirling a lock of blond hair around her finger.

George frowned at her cousin, confused. "What do you mean?"

Bess tucked her hair behind her ear. "The Green Club is an *environmental* club, right? Would an environmentalist kill a squirrel to make a point?"

Disappointment flashed across George's eyes—another lead gone—but then she turned defiant. "Maybe the squirrel died of natural causes, and the Green Club just took advantage!"

Bess groaned, and I held up my hand, speaking my thoughts. "Or maybe it wasn't an environmentalist who sent the note. It didn't say anything 'green,' really—just that there will be more trouble if Carrie doesn't quit her campaign. Right?"

Both Bess and George looked thoughtful as those words sunk in. "I hate it when evil is winning and we can't even figure out who evil is," George muttered.

Bess and I nodded, murmuring in agreement. As I turned the case over in my head, trying to make some sense of it, my phone beeped.

I dug it out of my backpack, read the text on the screen, and then showed it to Bess and George with a smile.

HEY REBEL—BARNEY GAVE ME YOUR

DIGITS. MAJOR ENVIRONMENTAL ACTION

HAPPENING TONIGHT. MEET ME ON THE

FOOTBALL FIELD. YOU IN? ELOISE.

Bess and George read it and grinned, George gesturing furiously that I should write back immediately. I took the phone back and began typing.

OH I'M IN, I replied to Eloise. IN FACT, I RECRUITED SOME FRIENDS.

~

CHAPTER SEVEN

Up for Anything

"WELL, WELL, WELL." ELOISE TURNED AROUND
with a big, impressed smile on her face as Bess, George,
and I strode onto the BHS football field just after dusk
that evening. "The rebel showed up!"

"I told you I was committed," I said with what I
hoped was an enthusiastic-looking smile. "Hey, Barney." He was standing just behind Eloise and had
abruptly stopped his conversation with a Mohawked
girl when I walked up.

He smiled warmly at me. "Oh, she's committed,"
he said, walking over to me. "I knew it when I first saw

her! This girl will really help us change things."

Eloise wasn't looking at me anymore, though—her eyes had turned to Bess and George, standing behind me, dressed (as I'd instructed) in utilitarian jeans and T-shirts. "And your friends are . . . ?" she prompted.

"Mirabelle and Jackie," Bess replied, reaching out to take Eloise's hand and forcefully shaking it.

Eloise nodded slowly, taking it all in. "What unusual names," she murmured. I shot a pointed look at my friends; I'd said about the same when they'd chosen the false monikers on the ride over, suggesting they might want to go with a nice "Beth." Or "Jane."

George nodded fiercely. "What can we say—creative parents!" She smiled. "Creative parents raise outside-the-box thinkers, right? Mirabelle and I are totally committed to the environmental cause."

Overdoing it. I swallowed and shot George a look that said, *Cool it.*

"How does Katrina know you?" Eloise asked.

Bess and George looked at each other. I panicked a little; we hadn't discussed that on the way over, stupidly. But Bess turned to Eloise with a big smile.

"Our moms know each other from the local NOW chapter," she replied. "They really taught us the importance of being involved!"

"Mirabelle and Jackie go to St. Mary's," I went on, naming the Catholic school in Boylestown, "but they're really excited to help stop the sports complex from being built."

George nodded. "This may not be our school, but it's still our earth, right?"

Eloise nodded slowly. "Yeah. Well, okay, guys. Here, let me introduce you around."

She went around the small circle of what I presumed to be Green Club members; some of the faces were familiar from the poetry slam that afternoon. "This is Kiki, Justin, Derek, Sara, Alicia, and Carlos," Eloise said, and each of the Green Club members looked up and nodded or waved in greeting. "These are, like, the most passionate members of the Green Club."

Kiki nodded enthusiastically. "We're the core group," she added.

"Whenever I need something done," Eloise said, "something that bends the rules, maybe, and might make some people uncomfortable, I know I can count on these guys."

Barney nodded. "Because all of us are totally committed to preserving the environment."

I nodded slowly. *Excellent.* These were the people I wanted to get to know better. These were the people who could lead me to Carrie's enemy. "That's awesome," I said. "Well, me and my friends are up for anything. Really! Don't hold back."

Barney grinned at me again. "Oh, I wouldn't hold back from you, Katrina," he said, reaching out to pinch my side. I let out a squeal and moved away. I am about the most ticklish person on the planet.

"Um, but really," I added, looking at Eloise and trying to regain my composure. "Dramatic action is needed, don't you think? After what Carrie Kim has proposed, and all the environmental damage that it's going to do . . ."

Eloise nodded, looking a little *well, duh.* "Yeah, I

got it, New Girl," she said, one corner of her lips turning up. "You're totally gung-ho. Noted."

I could feel myself blushing, but before I could worry that I'd overdone it, Barney moved over to my side and took my elbow.

"So . . . what do you like to do besides this kind of thing, Katrina?" he asked.

"This kind of thing?" I tried to smile. "I don't even know what we're doing, yet, actually."

Barney shrugged. "I don't either. Eloise gets all secretive about this stuff. She likes to be the mastermind. Anyway: Do you like music?"

What a weird question, I thought. *Does anybody seriously not like music?* "Uh, yeah," I said slowly.

"Do you know the Boxing Badgers?" Barney asked, a hopeful tone in his voice.

I scanned my brain. I could sort of remember seeing a CD cover with a couple of rodent-type animals wearing boxing gloves. "I . . . know *of* them."

Barney's hopeful expression broke into an all-out smile. "Aren't they amazing? They're going to be playing the Bell Jar on Friday. It's open to all ages. Would you maybe . . ."

Barney trailed off just as I was getting the alarming sensation that he'd been about to ask me out. I glanced nervously behind me to Bess and George, who were clearly listening and clearly trying not to look like they were listening. Bess bugged out her eyes at me like, *Come on!*

"Okay, guys!" Eloise yelled at that moment. "Gather round! I have plans for tonight ready. . . ."

My body went totally limp with relief. I turned around and saw Barney looking at me awkwardly, but I pasted on a bright smile and gestured to Eloise. "Duty calls, huh? Maybe we can continue this conversation later? Like tomorrow?"

I kept wearing the same aggressively oblivious smile as I grabbed Bess and George and hustled them over to Eloise.

"*Nance,*" Bess hissed under her breath. "*Seriously,* you need to put that guy out of his misery and tell him you have a boyfriend."

"I know," I whispered, shooting a guilty peek back at Barney, who looked both disappointed and confused. "I'm starting to feel a little bad. But I also think he'll be more likely to share information with me if he thinks he might have a chance to date me."

George rolled her eyes. "The ethical dilemmas of sleuthing," she whispered in a slightly sarcastic tone.

"Don't I know it," I murmured. A small circle had formed around Eloise, who was holding what looked like a map and smiling eagerly. After a few seconds, Barney walked up and joined the circle, a few people away from Bess, George, and me.

"Okay," Eloise announced. "Tonight we're doing something that *some* of you may not be totally comfortable with. If that's the case, you can leave, and I won't think any less of you."

My skin seemed to tingle with anticipation. *What does she want us to do?*

Eloise took a deep breath and went on. "Tonight, our mission is to . . . egg *Mr. Karlowski's house!*"

The other kids started laughing and cheering.

It took a minute for Eloise's words to sink in. *Egg . . .*
a house? What does that have to do with Carrie?

I looked at Bess and George and could tell they
were wondering the same thing.

Eloise went on excitedly, "You guys know that I have
irrefutable evidence that Mr. Karlowski does not recycle,
even though he has access to recycling bins. It's a personal
choice, but we're here to make him see how wrong a
choice that is! I can fit three people in my car; Barney
can fit four; Katrina, do you have room for anybody?"

George actually had to nudge me to remind me
that I was Katrina. That's how stunned I was. "Uh . . .
no, sorry." I did have room for one, but I wanted to be
able to talk to my friends without censoring myself.

"Okay. Well, with Justin's truck, I think we all have
rides? I've marked Mr. Karlowski's house on this map
here. Everyone meets up there in ten. Got it?"

"Got it!" people shouted back, but I was still
stunned into silence. Bess reached out to take a copy
of the map from Eloise, with a big *X* drawn over where
poor, ecologically irresponsible Mr. Karlowski lived.

My friends herded me toward my car, and I followed like cattle, still not sure what to make of all this.

"Hey, Katrina, see you there?" Barney looked over from the small group he was driving to give me a hopeful wave. I shook myself out of my confusion to smile at him.

"Sure, Barney. See you in ten."

He grinned and gave me a thumbs-up, which I returned. Bess, George, and I arrived at my car, parked alone under a lonely lamppost. Parking safety: My father had drilled it into me.

I plopped into the driver's seat and slammed my door as Bess and George closed theirs. "You have got to be kidding me," I said, taking the map from Bess.

Bess clearly had other things she wanted to talk about. "That Barney kid is in love with you," she said, poking her head between my seat and George's. "You get that, right?"

I held up my hand to imply that she should stop. *"As I have indicated,"* I said, "I am aware of his feelings, but am choosing to ignore them for the greater investigative good. Now, what are we going to do here?"

George sighed, examining the map. "This seems like a dead end, Nance," she said glumly. "I'm sorry to say it, but it's true. I guess it's possible that the Green Club could still be working on scaring Carrie into quitting whenever *you're* not around, but if you ask me? These are a bunch of kids egging teachers' houses. I don't think they're nearly as 'dangerous' as they'd like you to believe."

Bess tapped her lip thoughtfully. "We don't *know* that, though."

I groaned. "No, I think George is right," I muttered. "We're barking up the wrong tree. What do you think—should we just bail? The last thing I need is to explain to my dad why I was arrested in Boylestown for vandalizing some teacher's house."

George sighed and looked out the windshield. I could tell she was as disheartened as I was.

"Here's the thing." Bess held up a finger, and her clear, confident tone made both of us turn to face her in the backseat. "We struck out tonight; that's clear. But there's still some weird stuff going on with the Green

Club. They're the only organization we know that has a definite issue with Carrie's sports complex plan. And we still don't know why Eloise had the BTA stationery in her locker, which seems fishy to me, to say the least."

I twisted my lips to the side, fiddling with my seat belt. Bess was right. But I hated how few answers we were finding.

"I say we keep going," Bess said. "We may still learn something that will be valuable down the line. And either way, Nance, despite my teasing, I do think it makes sense to keep Barney close. He definitely knows what's going on with this club, and he might tell you everything you need to know, if you ask nicely."

I looked at George. She turned to face me, and I could see that she saw the wisdom in Bess's words too.

"I hate it when she's right," George said after a moment.

I nodded and put the key in the ignition. "So it's settled. We continue with the mission and try to learn what we can."

Bess nodded. "Settled," she said, putting out her fist.

"Settled," George added, tapping her fist to Bess's.

"Settled," I said, adding my fist to make it a trio. "Let's just hope we don't get arrested."

Mr. Karlowski lived in a modest neighborhood up in the hills of Boylestown. I drove through the maze-like streets until I located his barn-red ranch house and saw several other beat-up cars parked on the street nearby.

"Here goes," I said.

I turned off the ignition, and the three of us unclicked our seat belts and climbed out of the car, trying to make as little noise as possible. Barney had climbed out of an ancient black Ford down the street and gestured to us to hang tight—and stay quiet.

"Little speed bump. We have a special ally showing up with the eggs," he whispered. "Stay put until then."

We all nodded and climbed back into my car.

"*Seriously?*" George asked, annoyance edging her voice. "She didn't even bring *eggs*? What kind of amateur hour is this?"

Bess looked amused. "Like you're some great expert on egging houses?"

"If you're going to egg a house, bring eggs. *It's simple logic!*" George fired back, glaring at her cousin in the rearview mirror. "I officially doubt that these guys are involved in harassing Carrie. They're not organized enough."

After a few minutes a brown SUV with tinted windows pulled up and parked right in front of Barney's car. We all watched carefully as the door opened and a dark shape climbed out, arms laden with full egg cartons. At first all we could make out was a dark profile, but then the shape moved to Barney's window, passing under a streetlight, and knocked.

"Oh *noooooo*," George whispered, watching intently, her face paling. "Oh, you have got to be kidding me. I thought this couldn't get any worse."

I looked to where she was looking but couldn't see any cause for distress; the shape had morphed into an older, bulkier-looking version of Barney. This version had dark hair cropped close to his head, and he wore a rumpled-looking button-down shirt instead of a T-shirt, but the resemblance was unmistakable.

"I should have known," George was moaning. "I should have seen the resemblance! Oh, man . . ."

I caught Bess's eye in the rearview mirror, but she looked just as confused as I felt.

"What's the problem here?" Bess asked. "I mean, besides the obvious Committing Vandalism in a Strange Town for Dubious Reasons problem."

George groaned again. "I went on a *date* with that guy," she said, pointing at Big Barney. "His name is Jake, and I'm guessing Barney is his brother. I think Carrie set us up, actually. It was a long time ago, but he's going to know my name isn't Jackie and that I don't go to St. Mary's."

I was already automatically pushing the key back toward the ignition. We could make a break for it, make some stupid excuse to Eloise and Barney; Mirabelle got spooked, or I really had to use the bathroom. We could get away before anyone noticed the resemblance between Jackie and this girl Jake once went on a date with. But then I was surprised by a knock on my window. Eloise!

I swallowed hard and rolled down my window. "You startled me!" I cried. "The thing is, um, Mirabelle *really* has to use the—"

"And this is Katrina!" Barney's puppyish voice piped up behind my car, and I turned to find him just a few feet away with Jake beside him. Both of them were holding several cartons of eggs now. Jake looked down at me and waved, and then, horrifyingly, knelt to look inside my car. "Nice wheels," he said, nodding, looking from the dash to the passenger seat. "Is this a two thousand . . . Hey, it's you!"

George cringed. She'd been spotted. And it was too late—my chance to bolt had passed.

My heart sank. *Caught.*

George slowly folded herself out of the passenger seat and opened her door, standing and smiling broadly at Jake. "Hey there, Jake," she said in a confident voice. I realized she was still hoping she could save this. "It's Jackie, remember?"

Jake frowned. He shook his head slightly. "No, your name isn't Jackie," he said. "Are you playing a joke? Because I'm sure of it. Your name was really unusual, for a girl—Bob or Steve or something. I know! *George.*"

George's face fell. Barney looked from Jake to her, still smiling hopefully.

"Nah, man," he told his brother, "these are Katrina's friends from St. Mary's. Mirabelle and Jackie."

Jake furrowed his brow. "St. Mary's? No, that's not right either." He put the eggs down on the roof of my car and pointed at George. "Her name is George, and she's from River Heights. We went to a party together. She's Carrie Kim's friend. Remember her?"

A pack of confused faces turned to all of us, pale in the harsh streetlight. I felt my heart plummet into my stomach.

Eloise was the first to speak, all her friendliness disintegrating as she turned her hard gaze on me.

"All right, *Katrina,*" she said, her lips twisting into a snarl. "How about you tell us what's really going on?"

~

CHAPTER EIGHT

The Ugly Truth

"YOU DON'T GO TO BOYLESTOWN HIGH, do you?" Eloise went on, her nose wrinkling in disgust. "That explains why I've never seen you during school hours. I can't believe I never even asked you what grade you were in!"

I looked uneasily at my friends. "We can explain. . . ."

"You're Carrie Kim's friend," Barney said, pointing at George with an angry expression. "That's what Jake just said, right?"

George looked doubtfully at me. "I—well, yes. She's my cousin."

A gasp went through the little crowd.

Barney turned his glare to me now. "You came up to me at the protest, asking me all these questions about how the sports complex would impact the environment, and the whole time you're working for Carrie Kim's campaign? Man, how could I be so dense! You were just pumping me for information she could use to crush us!"

I shook my head. "Barney, that's really not true."

"Then what *are* you doing, Katrina?" Eloise asked, folding her arms in front of her chest. "If that's even your real name? Since Jackie is really *George*, and I'm going to guess *your* mother didn't actually name you Mirabelle," she added with a pointed glare at Bess.

I took a breath. "I'm Nancy," I said. "Nancy Drew. Look, I'm really sorry. It was never my intention to mislead you guys."

"Really?" Barney asked, his eyebrow raised in doubt.

I thought about that for a minute. "Well . . . okay. Honestly, it was. But it wasn't just to mess with you or hurt your feelings. I'm trying to find out who keeps harassing Carrie Kim."

Eloise perked up. "Carrie Kim is being harassed?"

In brief, I told her the whole sordid story: the note at the block party, the manipulated recording, and finally, the deceased squirrel that arrived in the mail. Barney paled visibly at that story.

Eloise looked utterly disgusted. "My God," she muttered. "You must think I'm an animal!"

"No, I don't," I insisted, then gave a helpless shrug. "But I didn't know how committed you were to the environmental cause or how far you'd go to stop the sports complex."

Eloise shook her head, then looked me confidently in the eye. "I'm *very* committed to the environmental cause. And I'll do anything within my power—anything ethical, I mean—to keep the sports complex from being built. But I would never *kill a squirrel*. Jeez!"

I glanced at Bess and George, who looked just as sheepish as I felt. Okay, I'd totally misjudged this one.

"Anyway," Eloise went on, placing a hand on

her hip, "I believe in democracy. The voters get to decide whether Carrie Kim gets a town council seat, not just me."

"But," I put in, as an important detail came back to me, "you had some Boylestown Teachers Association stationery in your locker."

Eloise frowned. "Yeah?" she asked. "And . . . ?"

I explained. "The first note Carrie got, the one that was handed to her at the block party, was written on BTA stationery. That's what led us to the high school in the first place. The paper smelled of smoke, and I was thinking Ms. Meyerhoff might have been involved."

Kiki, the Mohawked girl, sneered at me. "Ms. Meyerhoff?" she asked. "Sheesh, you aren't a very good detective. Ms. Meyerhoff wouldn't hurt a fly."

Barney nodded sagely. "She's actually a member of PETA," he explained, naming the famous animal rights organization. "There's no way she would send you a dead squirrel. She's the most peaceful person you'll ever meet."

Eloise was looking more and more annoyed. "The stationery in my locker does belong to Ms. Meyerhoff," she added, "so score one for Nancy Drew, I guess. But I didn't steal it as part of some nefarious plot to scare your cousin. I work as her teacher's assistant third period, and I write letters for her sometimes. That's all."

Ahhhh. I glanced at Bess and George. *Score one for Nancy Drew* . . . so why did I feel like this whole experience had been a spectacular failure? I'd upset some perfectly nice-seeming kids. And most infuriating, I was no closer to figuring out who actually *was* harassing Carrie.

Suddenly a bright light turned on outside the house we were standing in front of, blinding all of us. A loud male voice boomed out from behind the light. "Who's out there? Are those eggs? Eloise Stromberg, is that you again?"

"Oh no," Eloise muttered, looking around at the dozens of eggs Barney and Jake were holding. "I can't get caught again. Scatter, guys!"

I didn't know what to do for a moment, but then

loud footsteps came pounding down the walkway from the house, and Eloise and her friends suddenly took off running in all different directions. Jake and Barney tossed the eggs on the ground, and Jake bolted down a winding driveway across the street. I looked helplessly at my friends.

"Don't just stand there," Bess hissed. "Run!"

I ran. Not gracefully or straight, but I ran. I took off down the road and then turned down a narrow alley that was brightly lit at the other end, implying that it let out into another street. I heard footsteps behind me and my heart squeezed, but when I emerged from the alley and dared to look behind me before I took off across a huge green lawn, I saw that it was only Barney running behind me.

"Keep going," he said panting. "The guy ran down the street this way."

So I cut across the lawn and then across the street, down a narrow, rocky footpath that led down to the parking lot for a local playground. When we were there, I paused to think about where to run next, and

I felt Barney place a hand on my shoulder. He was still panting, trying to catch his breath.

"Think . . . we're safe." He gasped, then collapsed onto the pavement.

I was panting too. I put my hands on my hips and walked back and forth, waiting for my breathing and heartbeat to return to normal. "How will . . . I get home?" I managed finally, casting a nervous eye in the general direction of my car.

"You'll drive," Barney said, sounding a little stronger now. "Karlowski . . . he's caught us before. He chases . . . until he gets tired. Which is, like . . . five minutes. Then he gives up."

I nodded. "Oh." Barney looked a little more together now—his breathing was almost back to normal—but he was still sitting on the ground, staring at the pavement. He ran a hand through his hair, wiping the sweat from his brow, and then brought up his other hand and cradled his head. He looked utterly miserable.

"What a night," he muttered. All his pink-cheeked,

smiley puppyishness was gone, and he looked older, and also tired.

It made me feel terrible.

"Barney, I'm really sorry I lied to you," I said, meaning it.

He shrugged. "I get why you did it, I guess." He looked up at me, and there was a spark of playfulness back in his eye. "It's just my curse to appreciate mysterious women."

I couldn't help but smile at that.

Barney glanced in the direction we'd come and listened for a moment. "I think it's probably safe," he said.

I nodded, and together we made our way back up the path, through the alley, and back to our cars. When we got there, Bess's blond head popped up over the roof.

"We think Karlowski went inside a few minutes ago," she whispered. "It didn't look like he even noticed your car."

George stood up next to her, stretching, and gave Barney an awkward nod. "Hey."

Barney nodded back. "Well, I'll leave you ladies," he said, looking over at his own car. "It looks like most of my passengers are back." He paused. "Erm . . . I'd say it's been fun, but actually, it hasn't."

I cringed and nodded. "Fair enough. I hope you have a much better tomorrow, Barney. You deserve it."

He shrugged and turned away. "See you around, I guess."

I glanced at my friends, and together we all opened up our respective doors and climbed back into the car. I put the key in the ignition, but then just sat there for a moment, sighing. "That," I said finally, "was not my finest hour of sleuthing."

Bess reached up from the backseat and patted my arm. "Oh, don't feel bad, Nance," she said encouragingly. "The stationery sent us in the wrong direction. We can take another look at the notes, and maybe the box the squirrel was sent in? Maybe that will give us some leads."

George was staring out the window, and she nodded and turned back to face us. "We've definitely been looking in the wrong direction," she said. "Whoever's harassing Carrie, they're bigger and more dangerous than a bunch of eco-loving high school kids."

The next day I was desperate to do something worthwhile. So Bess, George, and I all headed down to Carrie's Boylestown headquarters to volunteer. There was lots to do, because Carrie had to let several staff members go when she realized she couldn't afford to pay them. The three of us stuffed envelopes, handed out flyers near the busy supermarket, and updated Carrie's database of supporters. By five I was feeling a lot better and had almost forgotten the disaster that was the night before.

Carrie paid for a pizza for all of us, and we ate it eagerly around the big folding table by the wall.

"It feels like we're making some headway," Julia said brightly, looking up from her laptop to take a quick sip of diet soda. "I just confirmed five new friends on Facebook!"

But Carrie's face remained inscrutable. "Great," she said sarcastically, pulling the crust off her pizza. "That *almost* makes up for the five hundred or so we've lost since the whole recording debacle."

Julia frowned. "Carrie, you have to stay positive," she urged.

Carrie put down her pizza and took in a breath. "I'm trying," she said. "But it's really hard when the front page of the Boylestown paper looks like this!"

She pulled a *Boylestown Bugle* out from behind the table, and I gasped. There was a photo on the front page from the disastrous dinner, with Carrie standing at the podium, looking horrified as the manipulated recording played. LOCAL CANDIDATE CAUGHT ON TAPE INSULTING VOTERS, the headline screamed. In smaller letters, the headline asked, IS THIS THE END FOR THE KIM CAMPAIGN?

Bess and George looked as surprised as I was. "How long has this been all over the papers?" George asked.

Carrie shrugged. "Since it happened," she said, folding the paper and putting it back behind the table. "But each time they run another story, we lose even more donors. It just keeps getting worse and worse. I'm almost out of money, cuz." She poked at her pizza and groaned. "I really wanted to do something for this town, and especially for those high school athletes. But I'm beginning to think maybe I should quit while I'm ahead."

Julia jumped up from her seat. "Carrie, no!" she insisted, walking over to her longtime friend. "You can't just give in like that. You care too much about this town."

Carrie shrugged. "But does this town care about me?" she asked. "They loved me when I was this big tennis champ. But now—I almost feel like the townspeople want me to move!"

"That's not true," Julia said. "Remember the elderly folks we talked to at the senior center yesterday? They loved your idea of bringing elderly volunteers into the schools."

Carrie blinked, then nodded slowly. "Meeting with them was probably the one good point in my last week," she agreed.

Julia narrowed her eyes. "And kids still like the sports complex idea," she went on, as if speaking her thoughts as they came to her, "plus lots of parents. That's still a really good idea, Car—some yahoo with a squirrel issue notwithstanding."

Julia seemed to be going deeper and deeper into her own thoughts. Carrie looked over at George, shrugged, and took a bite of pizza. "Too bad good ideas don't pay the bills," she muttered, sipping her soda.

Julia's eyes widened. "That's IT!" she shouted, loud enough to make us all jump. We looked at her curiously.

"Why can't a good idea pay the bills?" Julia asked, running back to her laptop and typing furiously. "The sports complex is still the best idea you have. What we need to do is throw a big event to get the town back on our side!"

"A big event?" Carrie asked disbelievingly. "Jules, have you not been listening? We don't have money to *pay the bills*. Much less throw some big event!"

I looked at my friends and noticed that Bess's

expression had turned all moony and thoughtful. *Uh-oh.*

"She's right," said Bess, standing up and smiling in Julia's direction. "The high school athletes still support Carrie, and the town supports them."

Julia looked up at Bess like she'd just invented the lightbulb. "That gives me an *amazing* idea!" She stood, throwing her arms out to either side. "What if we throw a joint fund-raiser for the campaign and for the football team? We could split the profits fifty-fifty and have some football players come make speeches in support of Carrie. You know they would, Car. This could totally save your campaign!"

I had to admit, it sounded like a great idea. But when I looked over at Carrie, she still looked hesitant.

"I . . . it's a good idea, Julia," she said, looking down at the table and sighing before she turned back to us and went on. "But how am I going to pay for it? I'm going to have to borrow money. And then what if it doesn't work? Not only is my campaign over, but I'm in debt."

Julia moved in closer. "Come on, Carrie. It's a gamble, I know. . . ."

"But it's a *good* gamble," Bess put in. She moved closer, nodding her head. "Trust us, Carrie—this is a safe bet. It's a *really* good idea. If all goes as planned, it could not only save your campaign but get you elected—and isn't that the most important goal?"

Carrie still didn't look convinced. But I could see from her thoughtful expression that she was beginning to consider it. "I guess I could ask my dad for a loan. Short-term, to be paid back as soon as the fund-raiser is over," she murmured, then shook her head and pushed her pizza away. She looked at George. "Cuz, what do you think? You have a good head on your shoulders, and I feel like I'm not in my right mind right now. Is this a good idea, or is it just going to make things worse?"

George looked from Julia's and Bess's expectant faces to Carrie's thoughtful one. Then she smiled.

"It *is* a good idea," she said. "Athletes love you, and why shouldn't they? I really think it could save your campaign, Carrie."

Carrie broke into a wide, bright smile. I couldn't help but smile too.

"It's official, then?" Julia asked, pulling her smartphone out of her pocket. "I can start making calls?"

Carrie nodded and stood. "And I should call my dad now. But yes, ladies: It's *on!*"

We all whooped and cheered, and Julia got right on her computer, searching out the best venue and athletes to contact and caterer to serve.

After the excitement died down, I returned to my job sticking mailing labels on flyers and putting them in a bin to mail. The thrill of a few moments earlier had passed, replaced by a restless, itchy concern. Carrie was borrowing money to throw this fund-raiser, and the last fund-raiser hadn't exactly gone according to plan. We still hadn't caught whoever was behind all the harassment.

I sure hope this works, I thought.

CHAPTER NINE

Unexpected Guests

"WELL, WELL, WELL." MY BOYFRIEND, NED, stood on our stoop, holding a red rose corsage and with a big smile on his face. He looked so handsome in his gray flannel suit with a tie to match my red shift dress. I grinned at him, leaning in to accept the corsage and a kiss on the cheek. "You *do* clean up well," he added, smiling even bigger.

"You prefer this to my usual polo shirt and khakis?" I asked, spinning in a quick circle. I did feel pretty that night; Hannah had helped me arrange my wild red hair into a complicated French-braid updo. And I was wearing a ruby pendant my dad had loaned me, which had belonged to my mom.

"I don't prefer either," Ned said, holding out his arm. "It's just nice to see you. I've been so crazed studying for midterms this week, I've barely had a chance to turn on Skype."

I couldn't say I hadn't noticed. Ned was a student at River Heights University, and I was used to him disappearing into little study hazes whenever midterms or finals were coming around. He was always so sweet and attentive when we *were* together, though—seriously, the sweetest guy ever—I didn't mind.

"It's nice to see you, too," I said now, touching his check.

"Ahem." My father's throat-clearing broke the moment. We both turned to find him standing in the doorway, arms folded. His eyes softened a bit when he saw me. "You look beautiful, honey."

"Thanks, Dad." I gestured to the pendant on my neck, and he nodded, his eyes misting briefly.

Then he turned to Ned. "Back by eleven, you two?"

Ned nodded. "Of course. We'll call or text if anything comes up."

Dad smiled. "Have a good time." He closed the door behind us, and Ned put his arm around me and led me to his car.

"So," he said, once we were buckled up and the engine was running. "Tell me."

I'd filled Ned in a little bit about the Carrie case when I'd called to invite him to the fund-raiser. But I'd really only said that the investigation up to this point had been a disaster, and Carrie was hoping this event could save her campaign. Now I went into more detail, telling him about the notes, the stationery that led me to BHS, the whole Green Club debacle. (I treaded sort of lightly around the Barney issue, though—just mentioning that he was a "nice guy" that I hated to deceive. No need to make him jealous.) I finished up with the current state of Carrie's campaign and what she was hoping the fund-raiser would do. By the time I'd finished, we were pulling into the parking lot of the Elks Lodge.

"Wow," Ned said, a little breathless. "This has been

one action-packed week for you, Nance. Did you actually egg that teacher's house?"

I shook my head. "No eggs were thrown," I said, "but I would have done what I had to do to keep my cover."

Ned nodded appreciatively. "Hardcore," he said. "But I'm glad you didn't get arrested. What if your dad somehow blamed me?"

I rolled my eyes at him. "Ned, come on. Dad knows I'm the firecracker in this relationship."

He smiled, and I looked out the window, watching people pull into the lot and climb out of their cars—a mix of young and old, high school athletes and their dates and supporters, plus parents, seniors, even a few local politicians. Did one of these people mean Carrie harm? I shuddered at the thought. Nothing unusual had happened since the dead squirrel's arrival—but I still had the sense this wasn't over.

"I just wish I had a lead," I said now, knowing that Ned would follow my thinking.

Ned squeezed my shoulder. "You'll figure it out, Nancy. You always do." He unclipped his seat belt and opened his door. "Shall we? You stay there; I'll give you a hand."

I stayed put, watching the dressed-up people come and go as Ned walked around and opened my door.

"And they say chivalry is dead," I said as Ned reached down for my hand and helped me out of the car.

"*They* don't know *me*," he said with a grin.

We had to walk around to the front of the building to reach the entrance. Even before we got out of the lot, I could tell something unusual was happening. There was something electric in the air, and the event-goers in front of us were whispering and pointing, letting out the occasional, "OMG!" or *"Really?"*

"What's going on?" Ned asked. The line to get in was sort of stuck—the older couple in front of us explained that the police weren't letting anyone in. Something had happened to the lodge entrance.

"Something?" I asked, craning my neck to see. "Oh, I don't like the sound of that. Come on."

I led Ned out of line and off the sidewalk, tromping across the lawn in my spiky heels to get around the building and get a good view of the entrance. Now I noticed Boylestown PD cars parked haphazardly near the entrance, their lights still flashing. Four or five policemen were standing in front of the glass doors, roping it off. *Oh no . . .*

That's when I saw the blood, and my heart stopped. It was bright red, poured all over the glass doors and down the stairs leading up to them. I raised my hand to my lips, feeling light-headed—

"It's paint," Ned said, running up beside me and putting a hand on my back. "Smell it."

I inhaled and could smell the chemical latex smell of paint. Ned was right; I felt a weight lift off me. *At least no one was hurt.* But this was still a pretty powerful act of vandalism. I followed the trail of red paint down the front path and saw a message scrawled there in the paint:

THIS REPRESENTS THE BLOOD
OF THE ANIMALS YOU'LL KILL BY
DESTROYING THEIR HABITAT!

The handwriting had the same block-style letters from both of the notes.

That's when I noticed Julia, down on her hands and knees on the path with a bucket of soapy water, trying to scrub off the paint. Her hair had escaped its complicated updo and was poking out in all directions, making her look a little crazy. Her chic yellow dress was smeared with paint and soaked with soapy water. She looked a mess.

I glanced back at Ned, then moved closer. "Julia?"

A man with a mustache moved in from the other side, pointing his smartphone toward Julia. "Ms. Jacobs, would you say this act of vandalism is a statement *against* Ms. Kim's controversial plan to build a sports complex on the site of a hundred-year-old forest?"

Julia stopped scrubbing and turned to face the reporter with an incredulous look. "Ya *think*?" she spit at him, shaking her head as she turned back to her scrubbing.

"Ms. Jacobs." A slight Latina woman approached

with a notebook and pen. "Will you call off the fund-raising event tonight?"

Julia sighed and sat back on her heels, blowing her escaped bangs out of her face. "Does it matter?" I heard her mutter.

The two reporters looked at each other. "Can you repeat that?" the man asked, jabbing his smartphone closer.

I moved in closer, not liking the sound of this. "Wait, Julia—"

But if she heard me, she gave no indication. "Does it *matter*?" she asked, looking from reporter to reporter, and then turning her gaze back to the red-soaked glass doors where police still swarmed. "This is a disaster. I've given everything to this campaign, but we're broke, we're losing in the polls. . . ."

"Julia," I hissed through my teeth, reaching down to grab her arm. Clearly all the stress was getting to her. Julia was a genius PR rep; she knew better than to air the campaign's dirty laundry in front of the press.

"Why don't you come with me? We can go to the ladies' room to freshen up."

Julia looked at me blankly. "They won't let us in," she said in a small voice, "because of the vandalism. Didn't you see?" She pointed to the front door.

Like I could have missed that. "Julia, I think you should stop talking to these reporters before you say something you regret," I whispered. "You're obviously really upset—with good reason."

I felt a gentle poke in my back and turned to find Bess and George—both dressed to the nines and both looking as baffled and disappointed as I felt.

"Hey, Nance," George said, smoothing her green halter dress. "They're starting to let people in the side door. The event is still a go."

I looked at Julia. "Did you hear that? You should go inside."

Julia nodded slowly, then pointed halfheartedly to her scrubbing bucket. "I should keep—"

"I'll take over," I said crisply, shooting Bess and George a meaningful look. "I'll make sure someone takes care of it. Bess and George will take you inside to find Carrie. I'm sure she needs you."

Julia looked at me, her expression dazed. After what seemed like an eternity, she nodded. "Okay," she said, dropping the sponge she still held back into the bucket and taking George's hand.

The mustached reporter pushed his smartphone after her departing form. "Any last comments?"

"*No,*" I said, at the same time Julia replied, "This campaign is a *nightmare*!"

I tried to stifle a groan as the reporters turned to each other with glee, the woman scribbling furiously.

Ned was waiting for me where I'd left him, just a few feet from where we'd spotted Julia. "Are you okay?" he asked.

"Not really," I replied. "I think this whole vandalism thing has made Carrie's campaign manager go crazy, and none of this is going to help Carrie."

Ned nodded sympathetically. "What do you want to do?"

I shrugged. "I guess we should go in—"

But before I could finish the thought, I spotted a familiar face, skulking off to the side of the building, away from all of the chaos. Dark mop of hair, nose ring. *Barney!* My heart squeezed, and I felt blood rushing in my ears. *What is he doing here? Skulking around like that?*

I reached out a feeble hand to touch Ned's arm. "Excuse me for just a sec. . . ." Then I went running over to Barney.

"Hey!" I yelled, wanting to make sure he knew I saw him, before he could dash off. "What are you doing here?"

Barney looked up. It was definitely him, though the expression he wore now—wariness, distrust, annoyance—made him look nothing like the puppyish boy I'd gotten to know. His eyes narrowed as I stepped closer, and when I was just a few feet away, I could see that he was holding a duffel bag.

He stared at me challengingly.

"What are you doing here?" I repeated.

His mouth twisted into a sneer. "That's really none of your business," he replied, and just as I was beginning to wonder what accounted for the change in his demeanor, he added, "You look awfully fancy tonight—you and your *boyfriend*."

I sighed. *Oh. Right.* "I'm sorry. Maybe I should have told you about Ned. It just didn't seem . . . relevant."

Barney shrugged. "Why should I be surprised? You lied about everything else."

I bit back a retort that I'd never actually lied to him about having a boyfriend—I'd just neglected to mention Ned—as I realized I was getting sidetracked. "It just seems kind of convenient that you're walking by with a duffel bag, after someone just spread red paint and an environmental message all over the front entrance."

Barney's eyes blazed. "What are you accusing me of? I'm just standing here!"

"With a duffel bag," I added, cutting my eyes toward the zipped-up bundle.

Barney snorted. "That's not a crime."

"You're right, it's not. So why not let me see what's inside?" I suggested, nodding at the bag.

The anger in Barney's eyes blazed even brighter—

it was safe to say, at this point, that it had turned to hatred. A little part of me felt bad, and saddened to lose a friend, but if Barney was behind the attacks on Carrie's campaign, I was going to stop him—right here, right now.

"I don't have to show you anything," he snapped, yanking the bag behind him.

I gave him a dubious look. "You don't have to," I agreed. "But if I get the attention of some of those officers over there, and *they* asked you, that would be a different story. . . ."

Barney groaned. He pulled the bag out from behind him and shoved it toward me. "Fine. If you're that convinced I'm some kind of criminal, knock yourself out."

I hesitated. His sudden giving in made me pause—it seemed like a bad sign. And I was right. When I unzipped the bag and hastily searched through, I found not red paint, but—

"Clothes?" I looked up at Barney with a confused expression.

"A uniform, actually." Barney reached in and pulled

out a formal black pair of pants and a creased, recently ironed white shirt. "I'm waiting tables at this event."

Ohhhh. I felt my heart jump into my throat. "I—I'm really—"

"Sorry, I know." Barney zipped up the bag and pulled it away, a sardonic smile on his face. "You've been saying that a lot lately."

With those words, he hoisted the bag over his shoulder and headed over to a side entrance. I stood watching him for a few moments, wishing a hole would open up beneath my feet that I could crawl into. *Another stellar interrogation in the life of Nancy Drew, World's Worst Detective,* I thought with a groan.

I spotted a bench off to the right of the entrance Barney had disappeared into, and collapsed onto it, taking a moment to collect myself. Why had I spent this entire investigation jumping to the wrong conclusions? First the stationery led us in the wrong direction. . . . That's when an unwelcome thought crept into my mind.

The stationery.

If Barney is Eloise's friend, couldn't he have swiped some BTA stationery from her locker?

To lead us in the wrong direction? Perhaps to make us suspect a teacher?

My heart thumped. It was an inconvenient thought to have just then—but it kept replaying in my mind. *He practically could have grabbed some when I was there. Surely he'd had that opportunity before.* And then I realized something else.

If he's an event waiter, couldn't he have worked the fund-raiser where the manipulated recording was played?

My sleuth senses were tingling. I hadn't seen Barney at the first fund-raiser—but then I hadn't been looking, either. I'd barely met him at that point.

I jumped up and found Ned on his hands and knees, dabbing at the painted walkway with the sponge Julia had been using. "Oh, Ned," I said breathlessly.

He looked up. "Don't look so impressed. I'm not doing a lick of good. The paint is pretty dry by now. I think it might be a lost cause."

I sighed. "Thank you for trying. I'm sure Carrie

will reimburse the lodge for the damage."

He stood, and I squeezed his arm. "All done out here?" he asked me.

I nodded. "Sorry about that—I'm ready to go in now."

Ned raised his eyebrows. "Find out anything?"

I shook my head. "No. Yes. I'm not sure yet. Listen, Ned—" I looked up at him and cupped his face in my hands. "I need to apologize to you in advance. My brain is churning with a million ideas, and I may not be a lot of fun tonight."

Ned put his hands alongside mine, then leaned down and kissed me on the forehead. "All I ever ask is that you be yourself, Nancy."

I grinned at him, took his hand, and led him into the Elks Lodge.

See what I mean? *Sweetest guy ever.*

Inside, Ned and I quickly found our seats, and then I disappeared to go look for my friends and Carrie. I found them in a small room backstage, where Carrie was patting Julia on the back and speaking to her in soothing tones. Bess and George stood awkwardly on either side, looking like they had no idea what to do.

"Jules, really, it will be okay. We've done everything we can. Now we need to just . . . get on with the show."

Julia looked up at her friend, and her face crumpled. She took out a balled-up, mascara-stained tissue and gently dabbed her eyes. "I just keep thinking about what you said," she whimpered. "If I hadn't insisted, you would have given up your campaign last week! And I think that would have been the right thing to do."

Carrie took a deep breath and looked up at that moment, catching my eye. I could see the pain in her face. It must have hurt to have her best friend tell her she should have quit, when Carrie had just, finally, started to accept the fact that she still had a shot. "Julia, go home," she said after a few seconds. "I've got this. And you need to rest. Okay?"

George stepped forward. "She's right, Julia. You're upset, and it's not going to help the campaign. Why don't you go home, get some sleep, and come back to HQ tomorrow, when you've cleared your head?"

Julia looked from George to Carrie, then shook her head furiously. "I'm not leaving you, Carrie." She sniffled, then brought the tissue down to her nose and blew. "I'll pull myself together. But I'm staying for this dinner." She shot an angry glare in George's direction. "Your little cousin can't kick me out!"

George groaned and rolled her eyes, and Carrie gestured like she was about to say something, but I walked over and grabbed her hand. "Carrie—can I talk to you a sec?"

Carrie looked up at me, confused. "Sure, what about?"

I shook my head. "It could be nothing."

Carrie nodded, and I led her out of the little room into the hallway, down toward the kitchen. Inside, a crew of caterers were working at top speed to get salads and appetizers out to thirty tables of ten people each. Things were chaotic, and nobody noticed us watching as a stream of waiters walked briskly out, each carrying a big tray of salads high above his or her head.

"Do you see that waiter?" I asked, pointing to

Barney, who now looked all crisp and proper in his black-and-white uniform.

Carrie squinted. "The kid with the dark hair?"

I nodded. Carrie looked at me curiously.

"Do you remember whether he worked the last fund-raiser?" I asked.

Carrie frowned. "I'm not sure," she said. "I don't remember all the faces. But yeah, I think I saw him there. And it's likely; we used the same catering service." She gave me a quizzical look. "Why?"

I watched Barney disappear into the ballroom. "No reason." I turned back to Carrie with what I hoped was an encouraging expression. "Well, Bess and George and I probably should find our seats and let you work on your speech. Should we try to take Julia, too?"

Carrie smiled with relief. "Oh gosh, that would be great."

We went back into the little room, where I told Bess and George that we'd better get seated, and George convinced Julia to come find her table with us; Carrie needed alone time to psych herself up. Bess, George, and I headed back to the table where Ned waited; Julia took her seat at a table near the front.

As I settled into my seat, though, I watched Barney carefully as he emerged from the kitchen again, a pitcher of water in each hand.

Maybe I haven't caught you yet, I thought, *but I'm keeping my eye on you.*

CHAPTER TEN

~

A Surprising Speech

IT SOON BECAME CLEAR THAT I WOULDN'T
have to work too hard to keep an eye on Barney.
He was *our* waiter! Just seconds after we'd taken our
seats, Barney hefted two pitchers of water over to
our table. A few feet away, he seemed to spot me and
shook his head, like *I can't believe it*. But he pasted
on a professional smile and kept going, ducking his
head politely as he filled our water glasses. When
he got to mine, he wouldn't make eye contact at all.
When he got to Ned, he "accidentally" missed the

glass and got a little puddle on Ned's lap.

"Sir, I'm so sorry," Barney said in a smooth voice, grabbing Ned's napkin and going to swipe at the spot.

"It's fine." Ned grabbed the napkin and sponged himself off. "Accidents happen." But after Barney nodded and made his way back into the kitchen, he leaned over to me and whispered, "Isn't that the guy you were talking to outside?"

I nodded. "I'm sorry. I don't think he's my biggest fan—or yours."

Ned watched Barney's back as he walked away, shrugging. "Hazards of a sassy girlfriend, I guess."

I smiled, but already my mind was cranking on another idea. I asked Bess for a piece of paper and a pen, which of course she was able to produce from her huge purse in about five seconds. (I love having prepared friends.) Cupping my hand around the paper as the rest of the table discussed the latest episode of *The Amazing Race*, I carefully wrote:

Barney,

> *I'm sorry I accused you. I know you're not a bad guy. Forgive me?*

—Nancy

A few minutes later Barney was back with a huge tray filled with salads. He carried a little metal stand with him, which he set up on the floor and then placed the big tray on top of it. Without making eye contact, he began swiftly sliding a plate in front of every diner. When he got to mine I slipped the note into his hand.

"I'm sorry," I whispered, quietly enough so that only he could hear.

Barney disappeared again, and we all eagerly dug into our salads. Ned, Bess, George, and I were sharing the table with two Boylestown basketball players and their dates. They all seemed very nice and were interested to learn that we knew Carrie and were working on her campaign. George eagerly told them all the things that made Carrie the best candidate for town council, and I noted that now when George talked about the sports complex, she seemed authentically excited about it. *How things change!*

I tried to pay attention and contribute to the conversation, but my eye kept wandering to the door where waiters occasionally popped out of the kitchen. It was one of the quietest times of the meal for the waitstaff, because the attendees needed time to finish their salads, and entrées were likely already set out. At one point, I watched Barney come out of the kitchen, lean against the wall, and make conversation with a tall Asian girl about our age, also part of the waitstaff. He glanced over in my direction and I quickly looked down, not wanting to get caught. But even after I turned back to the conversation at our table, I felt his gaze lingering.

Finally Barney came to clear our plates. He didn't look at me at all as he grabbed the plate containing a good half of my portion—I'd been too distracted to eat. I kept watching him hopefully, but he never acknowledged me, and soon disappeared with the dirty plates back into the kitchen. I felt my heart sink. *Did my plan fail?*

But a few minutes after that, as Bess was telling one of the basketball players' dates about an *amazing* nail salon she'd found in Boylestown, Barney reappeared from the kitchen—this time carrying a tray of entrées. He strode purposefully to our table, still not looking at me, and began placing the dish in front of each attendee. He placed mine last, and before he pulled his hand away, he found my hand and shoved a piece of paper into it.

By the time I realized what had happened, he was gone.

The rest of the table was laughing at something Ned had said as I unfolded the paper and looked inside.

FORGET IT—NO BIG DEAL.

Five words. But it wasn't the words I was interested in, it was the handwriting. As I stared at the blocky, evenly spaced letters, my blood chilled.

It was the same handwriting that had been used on both notes to Carrie. The same handwriting as the message scrawled in paint on the front entrance.

I could feel the blood rushing in my ears. *I was right! Barney is really behind everything!* I'd thought he was so cheerful and harmless—how had I been so fooled?

Now I watched him emerge from the kitchen again and settle, leaning against the wall, with a good view of the podium. *Oh no,* I thought. The speeches were going to start any minute. So far Barney had made his point using anonymous notes, a manipulated recording, a dead squirrel, and a can of paint. What else was he planning for this fund-raiser?

How is he going to ruin it?

I wasn't going to wait around and find out. I jumped out of my chair, and when all eyes turned to me, mumbled a feeble "Excuse me—restroom," before heading off toward the backstage room where I'd found Carrie with Bess, George, and Julia earlier.

I shoved through the door, only to find the room empty. I backed up and looked around, and soon spotted Julia, standing with her arms folded as she leaned against a plain white door.

I ran up to her. "Julia! I need to talk to Carrie. It's urgent."

Julia narrowed her eyes at me. She must have gone into the restroom to clean herself up; her hair had been tucked back into its complicated updo, and her yellow dress was now wrapped with a peach-colored shawl, hiding the stains and smears of red paint. She looked nearly TV-ready.

"Carrie's not to be disturbed," she said coolly. "She's in this restroom putting the finishing touches on her speech. I'm sure we don't have to tell you, Nancy, these speeches have become more important than ever! It's crucial that she get the tone just right."

I was a little stunned by how completely Julia had reverted to her usual calm, responsible self. Wasn't she just sobbing a few minutes ago? Telling the press that "this campaign is a nightmare"? Did she realize that half the reason Carrie had to get the speech just right was to undo all the damage Julia had done?

"It's kind of an emergency," I said, looking urgently at the door. "Can you get her?"

Julia looked me over thoughtfully, then uncrossed her arms and took my shoulder. "Maybe I can help you. Let's talk elsewhere."

She led me down the hallway toward the kitchen, stopping just before the entrance to the ballroom. "Now, what's up, Nancy? You look like you've seen a ghost."

The words tumbled out in a rush. "I think I know who the note writer and squirrel killer and entrance painter is."

Julia raised her eyebrows. "You do? Who?"

I turned and looked toward the ballroom. Sure enough, Barney was still leaning casually against the wall, nibbling a fingernail and waiting for the speeches to start.

"It's that waiter. Right there—with the black hair."

Julia turned to look at him, then turned back to me with a thoughtful frown. "How can you be sure?"

I told her the whole story as briefly as I could. How I'd met Barney trying to find out more about Ms. Meyerhoff, and the whole Green Club misadventure. How I'd seen the stationery in Eloise's locker. How

Barney had likely been a waiter at both of Carrie's fund-raising events. And most importantly, the sample of his handwriting—which I pulled out to show Julia—which clearly was the same handwriting used on both notes and outside, in the paint.

Julia's brow seemed crease further and further with each piece of evidence. Finally she looked up from the note into my eyes. "Very impressive, Nancy," she said, nodding slowly. "You're a very clever girl. Thank you for telling me. You can go back to your seat—I'll take care of it."

I stared at her, surprised. "Take care of it how?" I asked. "We need to get him out of here. Who knows what he'll try next?"

Julia glanced over at Barney, then turned back to me, leaning in to speak quietly right into my ear. "I want to keep this quiet, Nancy. This night has already been a bit of a PR nightmare. I realize I'm responsible for that, and I'm so sorry, but I can't take it back now—I just need to keep the campaign rolling." She paused and gave me a serious look. "I'm going to call the police and they'll come get Barney. But I don't want to make a big scene, okay? We're going to try to handle this without any of the audience finding out."

I opened my mouth to protest, but then stopped. It *felt* wrong—not to see Barney led out in handcuffs, not to have my big moment of *I knew it was you!* as he was led out by the cops. But when I thought about what Julia had said, I knew she was right. I'd become involved in this case because I believed in Carrie's campaign and didn't want to see it destroyed. And what was best for her campaign was to handle this quietly, with little fanfare.

"Okay," I said softly, with a little nod. "I'll go sit down. But can you tell the police to hurry, please? I'm worried about what might happen if Barney's here for the speeches."

Julia agreed. "I hear you, and I'll tell them," she said, shaking her head. "The last thing we need is another embarrassing incident!"

I took a deep breath. "Okay. Thanks."

Julia actually patted me on the back as I turned and

made my way back to the table. When I sat down I looked back in her direction and could see that she was already deep in conversation on her cell phone. She gave me a little wave, then disappeared back into the hallway.

I tried to regulate my breathing.

George reached over and squeezed my arm. "You okay, Nance? Your face is a little flushed."

Breathe. Breathe. "I'm okay." I considered telling her what had happened, but the basketball players and their dates were all watching us eagerly, their faces warm with concern. "I—I thought I saw a mouse in the restroom. I *hate* mice. But it was just a dust bunny."

Everyone laughed, and before the conversation could progress much further, a tall, burly redhead stood up and approached the podium.

"Good evening, ladies and gentlemen," he said. "My name is Ted Gelman, and I play tight end for the Boylestown High School state champion football team."

The audience erupted in cheers. Ted was one of the three football players Julia had selected to get up and speak about the athletics program and how Carrie's proposal would change things for the better. I struggled to relax as Ted's speech continued without incident. He was self-deprecating and funny, and the audience was responding just as we'd hoped they would—with warmth and interest.

But when Ted had been speaking only a few minutes, I glanced up and my heart jumped into my throat. Barney was approaching with a carafe of coffee. As I watched carefully, he went around the table, pouring coffee into George's and Ned's cups. I demurred, and he nodded kindly and moved on. If he had any idea that I'd told Julia to call the police to take him away, he gave no indication.

Speaking of which, *where were the police?*

Ted finished his speech to roaring applause, and then a shorter African-American boy with dreadlocks stepped up to the podium. "Hi, I'm Trent Wickham, and I play defense for the Boylestown High School *state champion* football team," he began. Again, the audience greeted him with warm applause. Trent began talking about what the football program meant to him, how it had changed his life and his outlook, and I stared stubbornly at the clock. Then Barney, who was leaning against the wall again. Then the clock.

Where are the police?

My heart was beginning to pound. Barney might have planned something to disrupt the speeches at any minute—and who knew what that something could be? So far his stunts had just been meant to embarrass Carrie, but what if he'd planned something more dangerous? What if someone got hurt? It might seem far-fetched, but he'd killed a squirrel, for goodness' sake. Wasn't that one of the warning signs of a child sociopath—cruelty to animals?

"Anyway," Trent was saying, and I realized that five more minutes had gone by and I'd not heard a single word of his speech. "I just want to express my wholehearted support of Carrie Kim, who was an athlete herself, and her amazing sports complex proposal, which will change the lives of many more young people like me."

Everyone whooped and clapped, and I slapped my

hands together on autopilot. *Should I find Julia again?* But then I saw them.

Two uniformed Boylestown police officers, making their way along the side of the ballroom toward the kitchen.

My heart leaped. They headed toward the kitchen, and one of the cops said something to Barney, who looked confused. The second officer gestured for him to calm down, and then pointed down the hallway, like he wanted the three of them to go and talk elsewhere. Barney frowned but followed, still looking confused, and the three of them slipped out of my sight.

It took every bit of willpower I had not to leap up and run down the hallway, but I knew that in doing so, I would only make more of a scene. Still, I focused every hearing muscle I had in the direction of the kitchen. Maybe I was just imagining things, but I felt I could make out raised voices over the din of conversation as the third football player slated to speak, a red-faced blond boy, stood up.

"WHAT?!" The shout was brief and furious, and

definitely Barney's voice. I squirmed in my seat, but just then the football player stepped up to the podium, and the crowd began cheering wildly.

"I'm Frankie Ludlow," he said, "and I play QB for the Boylestown High School *state champion* football team!"

More cheers and applause. If anyone in the audience had heard Barney's shout from the kitchen, it was quickly forgotten. But then I heard, clear as day, one more outburst in Barney's voice.

"Aunt Julia—what's going on?"

I lost my breath for a moment. *Wait a minute—* Aunt *Julia?*

"And I'm here to tell you," Frankie Ludlow was saying, but he had to wait for the applause to die down. "I'm here to tell you . . ."

I got unsteadily to my feet as Frankie finally got the first line of his speech out.

"I'm here to tell you why electing Carrie Kim to the town council would be a *huge* mistake for Boylestown!"

CHAPTER ELEVEN

The Wrong Man

THE HOOTING AND APPLAUSE DIED DOWN immediately. A gasp went through the crowd, which immediately grew silent, wanting to hear exactly what Frankie Ludlow had to say.

"Carrie Kim's sports complex would *destroy* the local environment! Do you know how many unique species live in Willow Woods, in the trees she's planning to tear down to build a new football field? They'll be gone forever, people, they're not going to be able to live in a few scraggly trees planted on the current field!"

I knew I should run back to the kitchen and see

what was going on, but I felt like my feet were stuck in concrete. Frankie's face shone with passion, and I could tell the audience believed he truly meant every word he was saying. But who had arranged for him to do this? Julia had chosen all the speakers. *Julia . . .*

I turned around and spotted her then, slipping out of the kitchen with a look of pure pride and delight on her face. She seemed to catch Frankie's eye and nodded to him, making a *keep going* gesture. Frankie turned back to the mic, adding details about what the turfing process would do to local groundwater and wildlife.

I glanced at Bess and George. Their faces were mirrors of my own shock. *Julia,* I mouthed to them.

"So as I'm sure you can understand by now," Frankie went on, pounding the podium with his fist for emphasis, "while I support the high school sports program, I *don't* think that athletics are more important than taking care of the planet. . . ."

The police started escorting Barney out of the kitchen at that point. He was handcuffed, and while it was clear they were trying to be discreet, several eyes in the audience turned to watch as Barney was dragged out, still protesting.

"This wasn't me! I swear! I was just . . ."

Over the din of Frankie's speech, the confused chatter in the ballroom, and Barney's anguished shouts, I could suddenly make out another sound. Banging. Coming from the hallway where Julia had told me Carrie was "working on her speech" in the restroom.

"Let me out!" Carrie's voice was barely distinguishable in the loud ballroom. *"Frankie isn't telling the truth! JULIA! Why did you lock the door?"*

That finally gave me the motivation to pull my feet from where they felt welded to the floor. I shot a meaningful glance at Bess and George as I went, and they sprang up from their seats and followed me as I ran over past the kitchen, down the hallway, and to the restroom where Carrie was imprisoned.

"Carrie, are you all right?" called George.

"I'm fine, but I'm stuck in here!" Carrie yelled back. "Julia must have locked me in from the outside! And I could hear the speech Frankie's making. . . ."

Bess was already digging in her purse before Carrie could finish her sentence. Within seconds, she handed me her precious credit card. "You know the rules," she said, giving me a warning look. "No damage to the magnetic strip. I've already asked for two replacement cards."

I nodded. "You know I'm a pro, Bess."

The card slid easily between the frame and the edge of the door, and with a few flicks of the wrist, I'd soon wedged it around the bar that held the door shut and forced it back, picking the lock. I turned the knob and pulled the door open, revealing a red-faced Carrie—still holding the scribbled-on printout of her speech.

Before she could speak, I held up my hand. "Hold that thought," I said, shoving the credit card back into Bess's hand and running down the hallway to where Julia stood, watching the chaos in the ballroom with a thrilled expression.

"So I hope you'll join me," Frankie was saying now, "in *rejecting* the *preposterous* and *irresponsible* plan Carrie Kim has put forth. . . ."

I grabbed Julia's arm. "How much did you pay him?"

She turned to me with a look of surprise that quickly turned to pride. She grinned. "Why, I didn't have to pay Frankie anything, Nancy. I just offered him a personal recommendation to Bridgetown University, you know, Carrie's and my alma mater—and Frankie's dream school."

I narrowed my eyes at her. "What do you have against Carrie?" I asked. "I thought you two were best friends."

Bess and Carrie emerged from the hallway then, and Carrie caught Julia's eye. Carrie's face was filled with surprise and hurt, but Julia looked almost pleased as she folded her arms again and smiled tartly. I had just thought to wonder where George had gone when suddenly the sound system cut out, leaving Frankie near silent on the podium, tapping confusedly at the mic.

"Is this on?" he asked. *Tap, tap.* "Can everybody hear me?"

He turned to frown at Julia.

Carrie clutched her speech in her hand and walked over to Julia and me. Her cheeks were flushed, and her eyes were dark with fury. "You did this?" she hissed at Julia, gesturing to Frankie. "The notes, the squirrel? You're behind all of it?"

Julia did something really disturbing then: She laughed. A real, delighted laugh. "That's right," she whispered. "And you had it coming! Our whole lives, you've been treated like the golden child, having all kinds of doors opened for you because of your stupid tennis championship. I was always the smart one, but *noooo*, nobody cares about intelligence anymore!"

Carrie frowned at her. "What? I had no idea you felt this way."

Julia's easy laugh turned into a scowl. "Do you remember when we both applied for that job in Congresswoman Rudolph's office? I knew every word of her policies, had studied her every action on the Hill, and you *still* got the job—because Rudolph played tennis in college and thought you were some kind of kindred spirit!" She paused. "Do you remember that, Carrie? Do you?"

Carrie's forehead creased. "I do remember that, Julia, but I had no idea you were still so upset about it." She moved closer. "That's when you got the assistant job at your PR firm, and I thought that made you happy. . . ."

Julia's eyes flashed at her old friend. "You were wrong," she snapped. "I was sick over that job—and I'm *still* sick that people think sports are the be-all and end-all of achievement! Well, you've had your come-uppance now. You quit your job to run for office, and now you're going to lose."

Carrie stared at Julia. Her eyes, still filled with hurt, seemed to harden into tiny black stones. "We'll see about that," she hissed. "I haven't got my come-anything. The election hasn't happened yet!"

Pulling her speech close to her, she poked her head into the hallway. "George! Turn the sound back on!"

Frankie Ludlow had stepped down from the podium and was talking animatedly with his teammates, who seemed to have a lot of questions about his sudden change of heart. Carrie strode purposefully past them and stalked up to the podium. The crowd hushed at the sight of her. Carrie took a deep breath, then smiled a dazzling smile.

"My fellow citizens," she begins, "this campaign has been a long and bumpy ride, and that may be partially my fault. But tonight—now—before it's too late—it's time to tell you what Carrie Kim is *really* about. . . ."

CHAPTER TWELVE

~

Victory
Celebration

"OVER HERE, NANCE!" BESS GRABBED MY arm, juggling two huge blue clouds of cotton candy in her other hand as she dragged me across the parking lot gravel and onto the grass that surrounded the new Boylestown High football field. "Carrie's going to cut the ribbon any minute."

It was three months later, and summer had settled over Boylestown like a warm electric blanket. The grass of the new field shone neon green in the bright sun, and the crowd was oohing and aahing at the beautiful new bleachers and newly planted and painted field.

George was already standing in Bess's designated spot, and she took one of the cotton candies and pulled off a hunk. "I think Carrie made a wise decision to put the new field right on top of the old one," she said, looking across at the old forest where the new field had originally been slated to go. "It might have been more expensive, but she was able to save Willow Woods."

"Well, it helped that she was able to get Hamlin's Athletic Shop to sponsor the field," Bess pointed out, gesturing to the bright HAMLIN'S—FOR ALL YOUR ATHLETIC NEEDS! ads that framed the scoreboard and were painted along the edge of the field. "They covered most of the extra cost. And I was reading in the paper that the owner says his business is already up twenty-five percent since they announced the sponsorship."

I smiled. After Carrie had decided to build the new field on top of the old one, her new sports complex idea had gone over well with everyone—even the Green Club. She had easily won the election two weeks after the last fund-raiser, and so far she seemed to be loving her new position on the town council. The last time we'd seen her, she'd beamed as she told us about a new after-school literacy program she was introducing for the elementary students and how much they seemed to be enjoying it.

Now Carrie stepped up to a small podium erected on the edge of the field. "Ladies and gentlemen," she said, "it's been a long time coming, but I'm thrilled to announce that the new Boylestown football field and athletics complex are open for business!" She leaned down with an oversize pair of scissors and cut through a red ribbon that had been strung along the sidelines. The crowd whooped and cheered.

"BHS!" some students began chanting. "BHS! BHS!"

George grinned, turning to Bess. "Aren't you worried?" she asked. "With these fancy new digs, isn't Boylestown going to crush your beloved River Heights team?"

Bess shrugs. "They may have fancy new digs, but

we have heart. We always have." She smiled and took another bite of cotton candy. "Besides, I'm sure our team is up to the challenge."

I chuckled. "Come on. Let's find Ned. He was going to get us a cold drink." But when I turned on my heel and took a step toward the concession stand, I bumped into someone.

Someone tall and skinny. Someone with pale-green eyes and a mop of dark hair.

"Barney!" I gasped.

I hadn't seen my erstwhile Green Club colleague since that last, fateful fund-raiser where he'd been led out in handcuffs. I'd learned the rest of his story through George, and from the stories in the local papers. Barney claimed that none of the attempts to sabotage Carrie's campaign had been his idea. He'd just been helping his beloved aunt Julia, with whom he'd always shared a love of politics and justice. "Too bad he was playing for the wrong side," George had added when she'd told me the story over lemonade a few weeks before. I couldn't help but agree.

Now Barney studied me through his green eyes. He looked more like his old self—cheerful, unselfconscious.

"Um, hi," I said, trying and failing to hide the awkwardness I felt. "Barney. It's good to see you!"

He smirked. "It's good to see me out of jail, you mean?" he asked, tilting his head to the side. "The last time you saw me, I believe I was being led out in handcuffs."

I took a breath. "Well." I could feel myself blushing as I forced a shrug. "Bygones, right? Listen, I'm really sorry if I got you in trouble you didn't deserve. I've been following your story in the papers. I know now that you were just carrying out the orders of the bad guy—you weren't the bad guy yourself."

Barney nodded. "Yeah, that's one way to put it. But I'm not totally blameless, either. I didn't see how twisted Aunt Julia had gotten in wanting Carrie to be defeated, no matter what. She was making it sound like Carrie was this totally selfish environment-hating witch, when, in fact, Carrie was totally willing to change her plan after sitting down and talking to Eloise and some local experts. I got duped, I did some stupid things, and now I'm paying the price."

I nodded. Suddenly I couldn't stop the question that had stuck in my mind for months from bubbling out of my mouth. "Who killed that squirrel?"

Barney let out a little snort of a laugh. "Man, that poor squirrel. I found it in our yard like that, honestly. I think it fell out of a tree. Anyway, I told Aunt Julia about it while she was having tea with my mom one day, and the next thing I knew, she told me she'd sent a box making some 'big statement' to Carrie's headquarters. Believe it or not, I didn't find out the details until you told us the night we were going to egg Karlowski's house."

I let out my breath. *Wow, that's actually a huge relief.* My perception of Barney when I first met him hadn't been that far off; he was seriously misled and had made some big mistakes, but at least he wasn't a killer (squirrel or otherwise).

"You said you were paying the price," I realized.

"What does that mean? You're not in jail, obviously."

Barney shook his head. "Neither of us were given time, actually," he said. "They gave us both community service instead. The judge thought we both needed a wake-up call about what's truly important in our community. So we're both working with this program that brings sports into underprivileged communities."

I raised an eyebrow. "Sports?" I asked. *"You?"*

"I know, I know." Barney grinned. "I've had some choice words to say about athletes in the past. And for the record, I *still* think this school places too much importance on athletics." He paused. "But it turns out I'm kind of a killer hockey player. Who knew?"

Who knew, indeed? I couldn't help but laugh, imagining Barney chasing around a puck on the ice. *Well, good for him.* "I'm glad you're happy," I said honestly.

Barney nodded. His expression changed a bit, and he twisted his mouth to one side. "So, hey," he said. "Now that we're on good terms, if you ever have some free time for an organic, sustainable veggie burger . . ."

"Um . . . I . . ." As I struggled to figure out how

to respond to Barney's request, Ned did it for me. He slipped up beside me and touched my arm.

"Hey, Nance!" he said. "I've been looking all over for you. I signed us up to be partners in the Ping-Pong tournament in the new complex, and it's going to start in five minutes." Looking up, he seemed to notice Barney for the first time. "Oh . . . hey, man." Ned nodded. "Sorry, I didn't mean to interrupt. . . ."

Barney waved his hand. "It's cool." He shot me a look of understanding. "Nancy was just telling me what a stand-up guy you are."

Ned, bless his heart, blushed. "Oh . . . wow." He squirmed a little, then gestured toward the complex. "Well, shall we? This other Ping-Pong team can't beat us if we don't show up."

I chuckled. Ned wasn't exaggerating; we're both *terrible* at Ping-Pong. But it was fun to play, anyway.

"I signed up to play myself," Barney said. "I should probably find my partner, Eloise."

As we moved toward the complex, we ran into Bess and George again.

"Hey," Bess said, touching my elbow, "do you know where the Ping-Pong tournament starts? George signed us up to play in the first round."

"*George* did?" I asked, shooting my friend a joking glance. "Miss I-Hate-Sports? Miss Why-Aren't-We-Funding-Chess-Club-Instead?"

George shook her head defiantly. "It's not sports," she said, "it's Ping-Pong."

Ned nodded. "And guess what? You're looking at your competitors."

"Wow." George widened her eyes, taking us in. "What do you think, Bess? Do you think we can take these two?"

Bess's eyes narrowed. "Bring it on!" she said, then added with a laugh, "Ping-Pong—the sport that unites athletes and nonathletes alike!"

Dear Diary,

I'M SO HAPPY WE WERE ABLE TO FIGURE THIS
one out! Boy was I wrong about Barney . . . but I still
can't believe that Julia would do that to her friend. I'd
never want to hurt Bess or George.

I think I've definitely learned how dangerous
politics can be, and I'll certainly be staying out of
campaigns, at least for a while. I'm off to see if I can
teach Ned a thing or two about Ping-Pong! Until
next time. . . .